THE TRUTH WILL OUT

A LAKE DISTRICT THRILLER

DI SAM COBBS

BOOK 18

M A COMLEY

For Mum,
my guiding star, my greatest cheerleader, and the truest friend I've ever known.
I'll love you for the rest of my days and miss you every second longer.
And for Dex,
my brave, loyal boy — thank you for staying by her side when I couldn't breathe.
You were my strength when I had none.
This book is for both of you.
Love always.

To Mary, gone too soon but never forgotten.

ACKNOWLEDGMENTS

Special thanks as always go to @studioenp for their superb cover design expertise.

My heartfelt thanks go to my wonderful editor Emmy, my proofreader Joseph for spotting all the lingering nits.

A special shoutout to all my wonderful ARC Group, who help to keep me sane.

Thank you also goes to my dear friend, Clive Rowlandson for allowing me to use his stunning photos for the covers in this best-selling series. xx

PROLOGUE

He reluctantly scribbled on the patient's notes and inserted the test results into the envelope, glad that his surgery still used the old filing system. His hatred of working with computers was well known amongst the staff. They had pleaded with him to update the system rather than remain stuck in his old ways, but his argument had remained the same for years: "What if the computers go down? Where will we be then?"

Robert Morgan tidied his desk and left his office with his dirty cup and medical bag in hand. He gave the receptionist the cup and announced, "I'm off to see Mrs Evans. I'll go straight home from there. I have a dinner engagement this evening."

He could tell the receptionist was dying to know more about his social life; however, she had the sense to stay quiet. He made a point of never discussing his personal life with the staff, and he rarely interacted with them at all. He had rules and stuck by them. The working day should consist of dealing with the patients and their needs, except in most cases, he rarely did that either. He knew his manner was brusque at the best of times and often borderline ignorant at others. His lack of empathy and bedside manner were notorious, not only at the surgery but throughout Workington. It prevented people from registering with the surgery, which, in turn, made his life easier on a day-to-day basis.

"Goodbye, Doctor Morgan. Enjoy your evening," Lisa said.

"I will. See you in the morning," he replied gruffly, then left the surgery.

His black BMW was parked in its usual spot, close to the rear entrance. After depositing his bag on the back seat, he slipped behind the steering wheel and drove off, not giving the surgery or his staff a second thought, as usual at this time of the day. His main gripe, when he attended meetings he was forced to go to, was that the other doctors' conversations centred around their surgeries, mostly the shenanigans their staff got up to, not only at work but during their time off as well. What concern was it of theirs, or his? That sort of rubbish didn't affect him, so why should he show any interest in it?

Robert drove out to one of his older patients, whose daughter had rung earlier. She'd told the receptionist that her mother was unable to get to the surgery, hence his need to fit in a home visit on the way home that afternoon. He detested seeing patients in their own environments. Some of his patients' houses were the pits. What was it with older people who always used Vicks during the summer as well as the winter months? He struggled to work that one out. It was a smell that irritated him and generally brought out the worst in him.

He parked up outside the patient's terraced house on the outskirts of Workington and rang the doorbell. A woman in her fifties opened the door.

"Oh, hello. I'm Doctor Morgan. I've come to see Mrs Evans."

"Ah, yes. Come in, Doctor. I'm her daughter, Vanessa. Sorry to call you out like this, but Mum has been poorly in bed for a few days. I'm very concerned about her. I think she has a chest infection. She's hardly eaten the last two days. I've been really worried about her. She's not getting any younger."

"None of us are. Where is she?"

Vanessa stepped behind the door and allowed him to enter. He didn't suggest removing his shoes. Why should he? It wasn't wet outside.

"She's in her bedroom. Can I get you a drink?"

"No, thank you. Would you like to show me the way?"

Vanessa quickly shut the front door and then scooted past him to lead the way up the stairs. At the top, the smell of menthol hit his nostrils and sparked his anger.

"The doctor is here, Mum. Everything will be all right now."

Mrs Evans turned her head weakly to look at him. "Hello, Doctor. It's nice of you to come. I haven't been able to get out of bed in days," the old woman said, her voice sounding strained.

"Yes, yes. Can you tell me what your symptoms are?"

"My chest hurts when I cough, and my nose won't stop running. It's not a cold because I always eat well with a cold. I think it's something more than that."

"I'll be the judge of that, Mrs Evans. Can you sit her up?" he asked Vanessa.

"I can try. Come on, Mum, let's get you sat up so the doctor can examine you properly."

Vanessa struggled to get her mother upright. Robert stood back and watched, not offering to assist them. Why should he?

"I can't, dear," Mrs Evans croaked just before she started having a coughing fit.

He raised his hand and turned his head away to avoid catching any of the old woman's germs. It was at times like this that he preferred wearing a mask, like during Covid; at least the rate of colds and chest infections had gone down back then. He kicked himself for not putting one in his pocket before leaving the car. He opened his bag to see if there was one hiding in there. At the bottom, he found one that was still in the packet but scrunched up. *It'll do for now.* He slipped it into position, then stepped forward and placed the stethoscope on the woman's chest.

"Breathe in... and out." He did the same on her back and repeated, "In... and out." Taking a few steps back, he removed the mask and announced, "She has a chest infection. I'll give you a prescription for antibiotics. That should clear it up within a week or so."

"But Mum has COPD, Doctor. Don't you think she should go to the hospital?"

"No. The hospital is inundated with patients. This isn't an emergency."

"I beg to differ," Vanessa snapped. "Look at her, she can barely breathe, and you think that's not an emergency? I've never heard the like. I'm going to ring III and see what they suggest."

He glared at the irate woman, scribbled a prescription, handed it to her, and then packed his bag. "Very well. It's your prerogative. The medication will have you up and about in no time, Mrs Evans, but if your daughter wants to get you out of your comfy bed and to the hospital, then that's up to her."

"I'll call an ambulance," Vanessa said.

"Another drain on NHS resources, when I've already told you what's wrong with your mother and written her a prescription."

"I'm entitled to get a second opinion. My mother is suffering. The trouble with you doctors is that when people get to a certain age, you write them off. Well, not on my watch. I intend to make sure she's treated properly. Mum isn't one to fake illnesses. Look at her, she's suffering and deserves the best care she can get."

"She has received such care. I'm sorry you feel she hasn't. Do what you need to do. The doctors at the hospital will tell you the same thing. There are a number of bad infections going around at the moment, but if you're not prepared to take my word for it, then there's little I can do to change your mind. I'll see myself out."

"Well, I never. Your bedside manner is totally lacking, Doctor. I'll be writing a complaint about this visit."

He raised his eyebrows and left the room without saying another word. On his way downstairs, he paused to listen. He heard Mrs Evans pleading with her daughter not to make a fuss.

"Don't be so ridiculous, Mum, you're in a right state, and he couldn't give a toss. I'm not having it."

"I don't want the hassle, dear. Can you get my prescription for me and let this be the end of it?"

"You're impossible, Mum. You have the right to be treated decently by the doctor."

He continued his journey down the stairs and left the house, making sure he banged the door on the way out.

Bloody people! They think us doctors haven't got anything better to do than be at their beck and call every day.

Robert got back into his car and drove towards home. Halfway there, at a narrow point in the isolated road, his car was struck from behind. He hadn't even noticed the van approach him. He slammed on the brakes and stormed out of the vehicle. The driver was staring at him, holding his gaze but refusing to leave his van.

"What do you think you're doing? You bloody moron, didn't you see me?"

The man stared straight ahead, ignoring him. Robert moved to the front of the van and took a photo of the numberplate, then returned to the driver's door. It sprang open, knocking him backwards into the hedge.

"What are you doing? There's no need for you to be angry. You struck me, remember?"

The man, with muscles that would put a bouncer to shame, glared and marched towards him.

Robert's gut twisted. He hated any form of confrontation. He held his hands up in front of him. "Listen here, I don't want any trouble. Hand over your insurance details and then we can both be on our way."

The man's lips parted into a snarky grin. "That's all there is to it, is it, mate? Wrong. I've got other plans for you."

Robert saw the man's fist coming. He tried to dodge it but failed. He was knocked out cold.

ROBERT OPENED HIS EYES, not recognising his surroundings. He tried to sit up, but the restraints across his naked chest, along with the extra ones around his wrists and legs, made it impossible for him to move. "What the hell is going on here? Hello, where are you?"

He surveyed the room. It was larger than average, with old rusty shelving along one wall. Most of the ceiling was thick with mildew. He found the smell, another one he detested, atrocious, and it didn't take long for him to start sneezing. The snot trickled down each side of his face. He had no way of wiping it, not with his hands bound. He was strapped to a metal table.

What the fuck is going on here?

His stomach rumbled. He didn't have a clue how long he'd been there, or how long he'd been unconscious. Straining an ear, he couldn't detect any movement outside the room.

Where the hell am I? What does this bloke have planned for me?

He lay there, staring at the ceiling for what seemed like hours until, finally, someone entered the room. But it wasn't the man who had knocked him out. Had he been a hired hand sent to abduct him? The man wore a mask. He was about a foot shorter than the goon who had rammed his car and assaulted him.

"What's the meaning of this? Let me go now, and I promise I won't go to the police."

The man laughed. "You won't get the chance."

"What do you mean? What are your intentions?"

"You helped yourself, didn't you?"

"What? I don't know what you're talking about."

"Your sort never do. You make me sick. Most of the time, you think you're so much better than those around you. I'm here to rid you of your delusions."

"I'm a doctor. I took an oath," Robert said, his voice hoarse because of the lack of water. "I *helped* people. I continue to *help* them. It's part of my job."

Footsteps sounded behind him as the man slowly circled the table, each step as meaningful as the last. His laugh echoed. It was low and measured. "No, Doctor. You helped yourself. It was never about your patients, was it?"

"I... no, you don't understand. Let's discuss this. I'll make you see sense."

Panic thundered in his chest as the man paced menacingly back and forth behind him. The man's breathing was calm and steady, unlike his own.

"The time for talk is over. Today... you are going to be punished." The figure stepped out of the shadows and came to a standstill beside him.

The overhead light switched on. It was a fierce light that blinded him. Was there someone else in the room he hadn't noticed?

The man showed his hands; they were covered in surgical gloves. He was holding a scalpel in his right hand.

Robert shook his head. "Don't come near me with that thing."

"Why? Afraid I don't know how to use it? Nothing could be further from the truth, Robert Morgan. I can tell you don't recognise me. That's good. It means you'll go to your grave not knowing who I am or why I would want to kill you. Believe me, I have my reasons. Let's get started, shall we? You just lie there, nice and relaxed, and everything will go according to plan. Oops, silly me, I forgot to ask. Do you want a sedative?"

"Yes... I mean no, you can't do this to me. I won't allow you to."

The masked man took a step closer and poised the scalpel over Robert's chest.

"No," Robert screamed. "Don't do this. Why are you doing this? There must be something I can do to stop you."

"There isn't. I'm getting bored now. Just lie there like a good boy. All of this will be over and done with soon enough. Now, are you ready?"

"NO! Please, don't do this. I don't know what I'm supposed to have done wrong." Robert turned his head away, unable to watch what was coming. The pain erupted in his chest a moment later. He screamed for the man to stop the assault, but his pleas fell on deaf ears. The darkness descended not long after...

1

Sam Cobbs felt contemplative as she sat on the banks of Coniston Water, one of her favourite spots. It was a place she used to visit often with Sonny, especially when he was a pup. It had been three weeks now since she'd lost him. Gone... long before his time, thanks to an idiotic driver who had mounted the pavement. They had been out on their evening walk, heading home to Rhys and Casper. Her fiancé was running late that night and had told her to go ahead and enjoy her walk with her precious boy; they'd meet up back at the house.

She was listening to music at the time, not through her headphones. Spotify was playing quietly on her phone. Even so, it was enough to deaden the commotion behind her until it was too late. She usually walked Sonny on the inside of the pavement, but for some reason, he'd found something interesting to sniff near the kerb and was investigating it. He was still in the same position when a car travelling at speed hit something behind them and spun out of control. Every time she closed her eyes since that evening, all she could see was Sonny flying through the air, his screams etched into her mind.

Sam shook her head and patted Tilly on the head. The little border collie cross wasn't Sonny's replacement, but she had healed a piece of her heart that she thought would never mend. It was her sister, Crystal, who had seen the advert for Tilly, a little rescue pup who had been transported to the UK from a kill shelter in Romania. She was the sweetest thing ever. The only downside, if you could call it that, was that she had a tendency to murder her toys. Sam had spent a fortune on her sweet pup since the day she had arrived. Crystal had volunteered to drive to Wigan to meet Lily-Belle, the lady who had fostered Tilly since she'd arrived in the UK. It had been a long day for the pup, and she'd been carsick a couple of times.

The second Sam had laid eyes on Tilly and cuddled her that evening, she knew she'd done the right thing in giving the dog a new home. She and Casper got on great together. They wore themselves out running around the garden, enjoying their zoomies. Doreen, Sam's elderly neighbour who had cared for Sonny during the day while Sam was at work, had also taken to Tilly, and they'd become best of friends from the word go.

"We'll never forget him, will we, Tilly? But I truly believe he sent you our way to help all of us heal. Between us, Rhys and I don't seem to have much luck with keeping dogs safe, not after he lost Benji. But all that is about to change with you, I promise you, sweetheart."

Tilly looked up at her and then placed her two delicate front paws on Sam's lap. Sam smiled and bent down for a kiss. Tilly willingly obliged. Every morning, she gave the best hugs and kisses as she jumped on the bed to greet her and Rhys.

The moment of bliss was interrupted by Sam's mobile ringing. "Hi, Bob. How are you?"

"Sorry, I know you're supposed to be having a few hours off. Believe me, I hate doing this to you, but I thought you'd want to know about this as soon as the news broke."

She frowned and continued to stroke Tilly. "What news?" Suddenly, it dawned on her what he must be referring to. "Shit! Has he been found?"

"You've just earned yourself a Blue Peter Badge."

"Do they even exist these days? Is that you, showing your age again?"

"Maybe. The good news is, yes, Morgan has been found. The bad news is... he's dead."

"Bugger. Okay, I'm out at Coniston at the moment. It's going to take me a good hour to get back, plus a further thirty minutes to drop Tilly off."

"You could always bring her with you and keep her in the car while you attend the scene. I'd love to meet her. I've heard you talk about her so much over the past few weeks."

"All right. Just this once. It's still going to take me a while to get to you. You'd better give me the location."

"It's the old clinic in Workington. You know, the one that has been earmarked for demolition along with the other run-down properties on that road to make way for a block of flats."

"I think I know the one you're talking about. I'll be as quick as I can and meet you there. I take it the pathologist and his team are already at the scene?"

"That's right. I called to make Des aware of what was happening, and he was already en route. See you in a while. Drive safely."

"I will. I'll have a very important passenger with me. Christ, if it gets out that I've brought along my dog..."

"It won't. Anyway, if anyone asks, this is you putting work first despite being off duty."

"You're a good man, Bob. I don't tell you that often enough."

"You're right, you don't."

They laughed, and Sam ended the call. She gave Tilly an extra hug and kissed the tip of her nose.

"You're the cutest thing ever. Come on, sweetpea, let's get you a drink and settle you in the car. How exciting, you're coming to work with Mummy." She fell silent and thought, *Even Sonny didn't do that. God, I miss that boy so much. I guess I will until my dying day. As pet owners, we never truly forget the special dogs that come into our lives for a reason. I believe Sonny comes under that category.*

She wiped away a tear that had slipped onto her cheek and

opened the back door for Tilly. After securing her pup's lead in the seat belt fastening, she filled the water bowl and encouraged Tilly to have a drink.

Sam put the address into the satnav and groaned. She had misjudged how far away she was from Workington. It was going to take longer than she'd anticipated, unless she used her siren. There lay a second dilemma. Did she risk scaring Tilly with the noise, just so she could get to the scene quicker? Once she was on the open road, she decided to give it a trial run. Tilly seemed a little perturbed to begin with, then showed no sign of a reaction to the loud noise, so Sam put her foot down.

She pulled up behind Bob's car, checked if Tilly was all right in the back, and then went to the boot to remove a protective suit and shoe covers, which she slipped on.

Bob must have either sensed her arrival or been watching out for her. He came to meet her at the front door. He shook his head. "It's awful. His wife is going to be devastated."

"Crap, that'll be the next job on the agenda: breaking the news to her. I'm going to need to see what we've got here first."

She picked her way past the debris strewn across the reception area, most likely caused by vandals over the years. The front windows were all boarded up, making the area dark and gloomy. Bob led her through to a large room that was filled with the pathologist and his team. Sam stood in the doorway for a while, taking in the scene before stepping into the room. Her gaze was drawn to the man strapped to a metal table. A pool of blood lay on the floor directly beneath him.

"Jesus. Someone definitely did a number on him."

"You could say that," Des replied. "Come in, Sam, don't be shy."

"Sorry, I didn't want to intrude. What can you tell me?"

"Meet Robert Morgan, a well-known doctor in the area who, I believe, was reported missing a couple of days ago. Am I right?"

"Yes, that's correct. We were hoping we'd find him alive."

"Well, as you can see for yourself, that clearly isn't the case."

Sam strained her neck from where she was standing to view the man's wounds. Bile instantly rose in her throat. As well as the victim's lips being sewn up, he had a gaping wound in his chest. "Oh, God. Has he had his heart removed?"

"He has. We've carried out a thorough search of the property and haven't come across it as yet."

"Shit. Does that mean we're dealing with a trophy taker?"

"So it would seem. The question is, what are the odds that he's going to add to his collection?"

"Heck, don't say that. One murder at a time is enough for us to deal with."

Des grinned and shrugged. "I'm just putting it out there. The killer came prepared."

Sam frowned. "Prepared to kill him?" To her, that much was obvious.

"No. I'm suggesting the killer brought some kind of container with him to transport the heart."

"What? How do you know that?"

"Simples... the lack of blood trail from the room. Although a tech found some in the reception area. It might be the victim's, or it could belong to the killer. We'll run the necessary tests when we get back to the lab."

"Damn, yes, sorry. I should have considered that myself. Hang on, you're not suggesting this is about organ harvesting, are you?"

Des shrugged. "I'm wondering if he was still alive when this person, or persons, removed his beating heart. I think it's too early to dismiss such a suggestion, but what do I know?"

Sam thumped her clenched fist against her thigh. "More than most. He's a doctor, for fuck's sake. Who would do such a thing?"

"I take it you haven't been to a doctor's surgery lately?"

"No, I haven't had the need to go. Why?"

"Sitting on the phone first thing for hours to get an appointment is driving the public crazy, and then, only emergency cases are seen. It's getting totally out of hand."

"Ah, yes. I remember Dad telling me he had to wait several weeks to see the doctor, and by that time, the symptoms he'd had cleared up. I'm afraid I have to be at death's door before I ring my surgery."

"You're the exception. There are a lot of seriously ill people out there who have to deal with these frustrations day in, day out."

"I feel for them. What are you saying? That you suspect one of his patients has done this to him? Punished him for not having the heart to deal with his patients correctly?"

"Who knows? That's your job to find out the motive. All I'm giving you are the facts of what's going on here."

"I appreciate it, thanks, Des. Does he have any other wounds to his body?"

"Not from what I can tell. I'll know more once I've conducted the post-mortem. His arms and legs were bound, and he was strapped to the table at the chest. That alone would have stifled his ability to move."

"Held him in place while the surgery was carried out?" Sam asked.

"To a degree." Des shook his head. "Beggars belief, but those are the facts as I see them."

"Why here? Why choose this place to carry out the dastardly deed?"

"Because it's empty?" Bob suggested.

"Maybe. It's a shithole with sections of mould everywhere. The windows at the front are non-existent. It used to be a clinic. Did he work here?" Sam asked, thinking aloud.

"So many questions and so few answers at the moment, as per usual this early on in an investigation," Bob replied.

Sam surveyed the room and, for the first time, spotted something written in blood on the wall behind her. "Jesus, I take it they wrote that in his blood. No, don't bother replying. It's bloody obvious they did. Shit! DO NO HARM. What's that supposed to mean?"

"He's a doctor. A GP," Bob pointed out unnecessarily. "I'm guessing he's wronged one of his patients in a major way and possibly a relative has gone after him."

"Maybe," Des agreed. "I need to tell you that I believe the heart was removed with precision."

"Someone in the profession did this to him?" Sam asked incredulously. "Is that what you're telling me?"

"I wouldn't like to say, not just yet, not without having a closer inspection of the dissected area back at the lab."

"Is it easy to find out how to remove a heart via the internet?" Bob asked. "Or is that a dumb question?"

"I'm guessing either the internet or the dark web will come up with a clip or two. As far as I know, every question known to man can be answered via the web these days," Des said.

"Oh God, don't say that," Sam said, her gaze drifting back to the body. "I'm horrified by the thought of someone checking out a twisted bastard's YouTube page, where they have filmed another person removing organs from a corpse. Or, worse still, from someone who was alive at the time of the extraction."

Bob ran a gloved hand over his face as the colour drained from his cheeks. "Did you have to say that? That's conjured up all sorts of images that I know are going to remain with me for a while."

Sam and Des shared a look.

"It wouldn't be YouTube, but I get your drift. Are we done here? Do you need to ask any further questions?" Des asked. "If not, I want to get this chap back to the lab as soon as possible."

"Will it be all right if we continue our search outside, in the hallway?" Sam asked.

"Feel free. And before you ask, I'll get the results back to you as soon as I can."

Sam smiled. "Thanks, Des. I don't care what the other officers say about you."

He glared at her and tilted his head. "I think you and I need to have a quiet chat later."

Sam laughed. "I was joking. Just winding you up."

Des jabbed a thumb in Bob's direction. "That's usually your partner's job."

"Hey, you two, leave me out of this."

Sam smiled and pushed Bob out of the room. "Come on, let's see what we can find out here. Any idea how they got in?"

"I'm presuming through one of the boarded-up windows. It looks like it has been removed and then replaced to me. This one here." He pointed to the large board on the right-hand side of the reception area.

"How can you tell?"

He puffed out his chest and announced proudly, "Footprints beneath it, a few drops of blood, and some of the screws are missing."

"Wow, go you. When did you work that out?"

"I told him," one of the techs said from behind her.

Sam laughed. "I thought it was too good to be true."

Bob grinned. "Go on, admit it, you were super impressed for a millisecond, weren't you?"

"Pass, ask me another," Sam retorted. She should have known better than to expect Bob to come up with anything half-plausible at a crime scene. *Stop it, you're being too harsh on him.* She examined the area as her mind raced. "The intent was clear. The murderer chose this place for a reason. Until we find out why that was..."

"Yeah, don't bother finishing off that sentence."

She searched the rest of the area and the other rooms available on that level. Finding nothing of any use, she and Bob ascended the stairs.

"Shit, it stinks up here."

Sam withdrew a mask from her pocket. It did little to block out the disgusting smell. Bob went ahead of her.

He pushed open a few of the doors and tentatively stuck his head into each of the rooms. "Fuck, don't go in there. I think I've found the source of the smell."

Sam had no intention of finding out what he was talking about. She backed up, and they descended the stairs together.

"Overflowing toilets are stomach churners."

"Too much information. Thanks for that! Yet another unwanted image for me to deal with during the rest of the day."

He grinned an apology. "You're welcome. That might explain the mould in the room where the body was located."

"That makes sense. Right, there's nothing else for us to do here. We'd better break the news to Mrs Morgan before the press get wind about what's gone on here."

"I agree. Can I meet Tilly first?"

Sam nipped back to the crime scene and said farewell to Des. "We're off. Ta-ta for now."

"Hope all goes well with the wife."

"Thanks."

Sam and Bob stripped off their protective suits and put them in the awaiting black sack. Then she introduced her partner to the new love of her life, well, apart from Rhys and Casper, that was.

"Oh my. She's tiny. I mean, I know you said she was small, but bloody hell, she's such a sweetheart. Can I have a cuddle?"

Sam ejected the safety harness and lifted Tilly out of the car. "Stop kissing me. A word of warning: her tongue gets into every orifice; she's not fussy about where she sticks it."

Bob laughed as Sam handed Tilly to him. "Light as a feather. Hello, precious. Well, you've definitely landed on your paws finding a home with my boss."

"She'll want for nothing and is already the boss at home. Fortunately, Casper hit it off with her the second she stepped into the house."

"Do they snuggle up together?" Bob kissed the top of Tilly's head, and just like a snake, her tongue came out and she started licking him.

"When they're not haring around the garden. I warned you about that tongue of hers."

"I think I'm in love." Bob sighed and kissed Tilly's head again.

"Easily done with this one. She stole my heart the minute I saw her."

"I can see why."

"Right, I'm sorry to break up this love affair, but we have work to do. Can you remember Morgan's address? Is it anywhere near my place?"

"Nope, it's in the opposite direction. She'll be fine in the car for a little while, won't she?"

"I might need to stop off at a park somewhere to let her have a wee."

Bob held Tilly away from him. "You could have told me that before you handed her to me."

Sam chuckled, put Tilly back in the car and secured her once more. "I'll follow you. If you see any greenery on the way, pull over."

"I know just the place. Does she go on command? Have you taught her that yet?"

"Sometimes. Every command is hit and miss at the moment."

"Stubborn, is she? Not surprised—she's a female after all."

"Bugger off."

Sam followed him to the outskirts of the town. Bob came to a stop by a grassy verge no bigger than a small front garden.

Sam got out of the car and said, "Is this the best you could do?"

He grinned and shrugged. "It's the only place I could think of that was on the way. Go on, let me see if she follows your orders as well as I do."

"Ha-bloody-ha, no pressure then." Sam eased Tilly out of the car and whispered in her ear, "Don't let the side down now, go wee-wees for Mummy like a good little girl."

No sooner had Tilly touched the grass than she squatted.

Sam faced Bob and grinned broadly. "That's my girl. Watch and learn, partner. If a pup who has been learning English for only two weeks can follow my orders, there's no reason why you can't do the same."

Bob had remained in his car. His response was to raise his window without speaking.

Sam let Tilly have a sniff around for a few extra minutes and then put her back in the car. They set off and arrived at the Morgans' house ten minutes later. Sam lowered all of the windows a couple of inches. Luckily, it was overcast today, not as sunny as it had been during the week. She topped up Tilly's water bowl, gave her a handful of treats and locked the car. "I hope this doesn't take us too long."

"I can make an excuse halfway through and check on her; just give me the nod."

"You're a pal. Thanks, partner. Okay, back into professional mode."

They walked up the garden path that had several stunning rose beds on either side. At the edges were dozens of companion plants. The display took Sam's breath away. "I'd love a garden like this."

Bob shrugged. "It's all right, I suppose. Not really my cup of tea. I prefer something maintenance-free. There's a lot of work gone into keeping this garden in good nick."

"That's true. If only I had the time." Sam rang the bell.

Mrs Morgan answered the door within seconds. She gasped as soon as she saw them standing on the doorstep. "Oh no... this isn't good news, is it?"

Sam shook her head. "Can we come in, Melinda?"

The woman took a step back. She slid down the wall and covered her head with her hands. "I knew it... knew I'd seen him for the last time."

"Come on, let me help you up. We'll chat in the lounge, shall we?"

Sam held out a hand, and Melinda gripped it. She struggled to get to her feet until Bob offered to lend a hand.

"Thank you. I guess I'm not as young as I used to be. It's all right getting down there; it's getting up that's the hardest part. Shall I make a drink?"

"Not for us. Do you need one?" Sam asked.

"No, I'll be all right."

They moved to the large lounge, which had a modern feel to it—not what Sam was expecting at all. Melinda sat in the easy chair, and Sam and Bob chose the sofa.

"Where was he? Why did someone abduct him? Do you know?"

"Not yet. His body was found in the abandoned clinic in town, the one they're supposed to be demolishing soon."

Melinda pulled a tissue from the box next to her and dabbed at her eyes. "Was he gone when you got there?"

"Yes, he was already dead. We're not sure how long he had been there or why the killer chose that location. Do you have any ideas about that?"

"No, none at all. I'm not sure if he ever went there. I'm sorry, my mind is a blur. I can't think straight. How? How did they kill him?"

Sam always dreaded when a relative asked that particular question. "I'm going to be honest with you. It wasn't pleasant, but I really don't think I should go into details, not right now."

Melinda groaned and covered her face. She sobbed for a few moments and then dropped her hands and stared at Sam. "Don't tell me he was cut up. I couldn't bear the thought of him suffering while someone cut him into pieces."

"No, not exactly, although an organ was removed from his body."

Shaking her head, Melinda asked, "An organ? Why? Which part of him was taken? Oh God, please don't tell me someone stole it to help out another person? You hear about these dodgy backstreet kidney operations going on all the time."

"As I said, we're unsure how or why your husband was killed at this early stage."

"You haven't told me which organ the bastards stole."

After a moment's pause, Sam confirmed the truth: "It was his heart."

"That's sick," Melinda yelled. She rose from her chair, but her legs gave way beneath her, and she sat again. "Why? Was he alive when they took it? He must have been if they intend to give it to someone else. My God, I don't want to think about this, but I need to know. This is too horrendous for words. I hope Robert didn't suffer for too long."

"Without having the pathologist's report to hand, I'm sorry, I won't be able to answer your questions. I know that's little to no comfort to you at this time."

"You're right, it's not. What kind of warped individual rips out the heart of a doctor who has served this community well over the last fifteen years? I can't believe he's gone, and in the manner that he was taken from me. Do you have any clues as to who did this? I doubt if they left a signed confession at the scene, but they might have left some form of evidence behind. Did they?"

"There was a message written on the wall of the room where your husband was found, which read, 'Do no harm'."

"And what's that supposed to mean? My husband was a doctor. He never harmed anyone, not knowingly. Jesus, why has this person taken him from me? We've just celebrated our eighteenth anniversary, only last week, in fact. Now my life as I know it is going to change forever."

"It's too early to say why they chose your husband. Can you tell us if he'd received any threats over the last few months?"

Melinda thought about the question for a while, then shook her head. "Not that he told me."

"What about the neighbours? Any issues there?"

"No, we're quite friendly with all of them. Newcomers are arriving all the time, and sometimes it takes a while to get to know them, but I wouldn't say any of them are nasty towards us. Far from it."

"I have to ask, what about at the surgery? Had he fallen out with either his colleagues or any of his patients?"

Her head dipped, and she hitched up a shoulder. "I don't really know; you'd have to ask them. Robert wasn't really the type to bring his work home with him. He preferred not to discuss what kind of day he'd had, and I never pushed him on the subject either."

"It's the Hawsland Surgery, isn't it?"

"That's correct. Two other doctors work there."

"We'll pay them a visit. Are they aware that your husband had gone missing?"

"Yes, I rang them right away. They told me that my husband had visited an elderly patient on his way home. I'm assuming whoever abducted him forced him off the road after he left Mrs Evans's house."

"You gave us that information before. We've been reviewing the cameras in that area ever since but haven't come up with anything as yet."

"Where do we go from here? Can I see him, or is it too soon?"

"The post-mortem will take place over the next few days. I'll pass on your details to the pathologist. He'll be in touch when you can see your husband."

"Thank you." She plucked another tissue from the box and blew her nose. "What am I going to do without him? I left everything to him. He sorted out all the bills and was in charge of our finances. I don't know how I'm going to cope now."

"Is there a family member who can help you?"

"I have a sister living in Coventry. I hope this doesn't come across as being unkind, but she's worse than me when it comes to things like this. I remember when our parents died over ten years ago, she left everything to me. She struggled to handle the stress, so she'd be worse than useless if I rang and asked for help."

"I can appoint a Family Liaison Officer, if that will help?"

"Would you? I'm just lost. I don't know which way to turn for the best."

"Don't worry, we'll help you get everything sorted. Is there anything else you can tell us before we leave?"

"No, I can't think of anything."

Sam and Bob stood.

"Stay there," Sam said. "We'll show ourselves out. I gave you a card the other day, didn't I?"

"Yes, when I popped into the station to report Robert missing— that seems like an eternity ago. I've barely slept a wink since then."

Sam patted Melinda's forearm. "Hopefully that won't be the case today. Be kind to yourself and rest when you can."

"Thank you, Inspector, for everything, and most of all, for being kind to me."

"You're welcome. I'm always here if you need me. I'm going back to the station now. I'll get the FLO organised as soon as I return. Someone will be in touch before the end of the day, I promise."

Melinda nodded and leaned her head back in the chair. "Thank you again."

Sam and Bob left her to it and returned to their cars.

"That went better than I thought it would," Bob said.

"Still tough. Right, I'm going to shoot Tilly home before I go to the station. I'll leave you to fill in the rest of the team. I shouldn't be too long."

"Take your time, bearing in mind that you're supposed to be taking time off."

"That's over and done with now. We have a killer to catch."

They jumped back into their respective cars just as the rain started.

"How's that for timing, hey, little one? Shall we go and see what Auntie Doreen is up to?"

Tilly yawned. Sam sensed she had just woken her up. She was happy being in the car as long as she was with Sam.

DOREEN WAS EXCITED to see them, and Tilly was just as enthusiastic to see her. Her neighbour had also spent a fortune on toys to keep the pup happy during the day.

"Have many survived?" Sam asked.

"A few. Gosh, even the supposedly indestructible toys haven't stood the test of time."

"I'll replace them for you at the end of the month."

"You'll do no such thing. It's human company she's craving. I'm sure she'll settle down in a few weeks. Bless her, we don't know much about her past. It'll take her a while to get used to a proper routine. Did you enjoy your time at Coniston?"

"We did. We were chilling in the sun over there until Bob rang me. I've been at work for the last couple of hours."

"What? Sam, you really need to tell them no now and again and be firm about it. You rarely get time off as it is."

"I know. I don't mind, especially when I have another murder case that needs solving."

"My, oh my. What is the world coming to? Until I met you, I never realised how many murders there were in this area. I hope you find the person responsible soon. Can you tell me who the victim is?"

"Doctor Robert Morgan. Without going into detail, he met a very gruesome death."

Doreen stared at her and then slowly sank into her chair. "But... he's my doctor."

"Shit! Sorry, I shouldn't have told you. Can I get you a glass of water?"

"No, it's okay. Well, I never expected you to tell me that, Sam. How did he die? Or can't you tell me?"

"I shouldn't, but I know it won't go any further. Sadly, the killer cut his heart out."

"Did he have one? Oh gosh, I can't believe I said that."

Sam frowned and tilted her head. "What do you mean, Doreen?"

"I don't like to speak ill of the dead, but I don't think that man had a sympathetic bone in his body."

"What? Has he always been the same, or has he changed recently?"

"He's always been a bit off with me as far back as I can remember."

"Why didn't you change doctors?"

"You're right, I should've done, but I couldn't be bothered. The surgery is the nearest one to me, and now that I can no longer drive, I stayed with them because it was convenient."

"You should have said something. We could have worked around it. Blimey, patients have the right to be treated properly by their own doctor."

"They do. I put up with it because of my age. I've never been one for causing problems."

Sam sighed. "I can't believe you're telling me this. I hope his replacement treats you better. As soon as they take over, I want you to make an appointment and get a thorough checkup, you hear me?"

"I do and I will. Despite his ignorance and the way he treated people, he still shouldn't have been killed. Fancy removing his heart."

"I know. It didn't make sense before, but now that you've told me what he was like towards you, it does. I think we have a lot of digging to do down at the surgery."

Doreen cringed. "I hope I haven't opened up a can of worms."

"You probably have, but I'm glad you were open with me. This kind of information rarely comes out at the start of an investigation."

Doreen offered a weak smile. "I'm glad I could help out, without realising I had. What will happen next?"

"Once I've changed out of my civvies, I'll head for the station. I'm tempted to visit the surgery on the way back, but I think I'd rather leave that until tomorrow when my head is fully back in the game."

"You do what you have to do and leave Tilly with me. I hope you manage to solve the case soon, Sam. As much as I detested the man at times, he still didn't deserve to die, not the way he did."

"No one deserved that, no matter how appalling he was to his patients. Thanks for confiding in me. You should have spoken up sooner, though."

"I know. But I'm the type to just get on with life, you know that, Sam."

"I know, but over the past year I've seen a noticeable change in your health."

Tears brimmed Doreen's grey eyes. "And there I was thinking that I had hidden it well."

Sam leaned in and hugged Doreen tightly. "We're here for you, Doreen. Please, please always remember that." She released her and took a step back. Tilly jumped onto Doreen's lap and started licking her face. "Tilly, no. Give Doreen some peace."

"She's fine. She's such a friendly little girl. Go on, leave us to it. We'll see you later. Does this mean you'll be late home this evening?"

"I hope not. I'll give you a call if that changes. Thanks again for looking after Tilly and for confiding in me about Morgan."

Doreen raised a finger. "Now then, Sam, I know that look. Just because he was a bad man, it doesn't mean that you can deal with the case differently now. Was he married? I have it at the back of my mind that he was."

"Yes. Bob and I visited his wife to break the news earlier."

"Then do it for her."

"I will. I promise. See you later." Sam made a swift exit before Tilly realised what was going on and closed the door behind her.

Poor Doreen. How dare Morgan treat her and other patients badly? What was wrong with him? And a doctor, to boot. That's his job: to care for his patients, and over the years he's apparently failed in his duties. Damn, that means we could be dealing with a long list of suspects here.

2

Sam arrived back at the station thirty minutes later. The new desk sergeant was on duty and welcomed her.

"Hi, Jason, how's it going?"

"Pretty good, thanks, ma'am. Sorry you got called in."

Jason Collins had been at the station for years. He'd jumped at the chance to fill Nick Travis's shoes. Nick had joined Sam's team after the death of Alex, another team member. There had been a lot of sadness for Sam to contend with in the past eighteen months or so, not forgetting the loss of two dogs, Sonny and Benji. But that's what life throws at you at times. The good news was that she and Rhys had a wedding to look forward to in a few weeks. Her sister, Crystal, who ran a bridal boutique in Workington, had everything covered on that front. She'd told Sam to leave all the preparations to her to sort out. Sam had made it clear they were on a limited budget, and Crystal had agreed to bear that in mind. Whether that would be the case, she wasn't sure.

Sam entered the code into the keypad and stepped into the inner sanctum of the station, where the public was forbidden access.

Bob made her a coffee as soon as she entered the incident room and brought her up to date. "I think we should visit the surgery ASAP, if only to see what kind of doctor he was."

Sam took a sip from her coffee, then confessed to the team, "Ah, I already know."

Bob retook his seat and frowned. "What? You've already been there?"

"Nope, I think we should go tomorrow. I was chatting to Doreen, my neighbour, when I dropped Tilly off, and she told me that Morgan had been her family doctor for years."

"Wow, that's a pretty big coincidence, considering the number of doctors we have registered in the area."

Intrigued, Sam asked, "How many?"

"Twenty-odd. Saying that, the numbers have dwindled drastically over the last few years."

"Doctors leaving the NHS?"

Bob nodded. "Yep, and who could blame them? It's a bloody shambles, any idiot can see that, apart from the politicians, apparently."

"That's true. Let's not go down that route. Let's deal with the hand we've been dealt, eh? Anyway, Doreen told me that he was a bad doctor and often treated her appallingly."

"Wow, is that right? Poor Doreen. Did she complain about him?"

"No, because the surgery is the closest to her, and she's really not the type to air her grievances, as it were."

"People need to complain. It's their right to be treated properly by doctors. It's the doctors' job to care for people in their community. If he failed to do that, then he should have been reprimanded by the General Medical Council. Hey, I might contact them. What do you think?"

"That's a great idea. Yes, we should get in touch with them as soon as possible. Has anything come through from the CCTV yet?"

"Not yet. The incident happened out in the sticks; no cameras were available."

"Well, other than visiting the surgery, I don't know where else we can turn. What about the clinic where he was found? Any connection to Morgan showing up there?"

The usually reliable Claire shook her head. "I had the same thought, so delved into it. I couldn't find anything on record."

"That's not to say he didn't visit the place," Sam said. "Do we know what sort of clinic it was?"

"Alternative medicine," Claire replied.

"That could mean anything. Let's not rule it out yet. According to his wife, everything was hunky-dory at home and with the neighbours. Therefore, that only leaves us with one possible angle to tackle: a disgruntled patient, doesn't it?"

"Unless there's something going on in his past that Mrs Morgan wasn't aware of," Bob added. "And don't forget what Des said about the way his body was dissected, or should I say, his heart removed?"

Sam placed a finger and thumb on either side of her chin. "That's right. He told us the task was carried out with precision, suggesting that someone knew what they were doing."

Bob clicked his fingers. "What about another doctor? Maybe he's stepped on a colleague's toes over the years, and they've found a way of getting their revenge on him."

"By killing him and removing his heart? That's a little far-fetched, even for you, Bob."

"Worth looking into, if we've got nothing else to go on yet."

The rest of the team nodded their agreement.

Sam sighed. "Reluctantly, I agree. I'll leave you folks to it. There's bound to be a desk full of mail awaiting my attention. Let me know if you find anything. Our hands are tied until the PM results come through."

"We could visit the surgery," Bob called after her.

"On my to-do list for tomorrow," she reminded him, then closed the office door behind her.

She let out a weary sigh; so much for having some time off. The last few months had been full-on for her and the team, with no reprieve between cases. At least, that's how it had felt at times. Still, she had her upcoming wedding to look forward to, except, with the death of Sonny, she had to admit that her heart wasn't really in it. Although she wouldn't tell either Rhys or her sister that. Did she feel railroaded into marrying Rhys now? Her head was so mixed up, she couldn't answer that question. It had seemed a good idea at the time when he'd asked her.

Stop it. I love him. That should be all that matters, not whether the timing is right or not.

She stared at her post for a few minutes, not having the inclination to get stuck into the onerous chore. At the end of her unexpected deliberation, she gathered the brown envelopes together, dumped them in her in-tray and left her seat. She removed her jacket from the back of her chair and opened her office door. "I've changed my mind, Bob. Come on, let's strike while the iron is hot."

Her partner leapt out of his seat. "I had a feeling you would."

She smirked. "You think you know me so well. One of these days, I'll surprise the hell out of you and do something off the cuff."

He sniggered. "I doubt it. You're far too predictable."

"It's better to be predictable than... nope, I'm not going there." Sam glanced over at Nick Travis, whose mouth was gaping open. "You'll get used to the banter around here, Nick."

He laughed. "Will I?"

Sam winked, and she shoved Bob in the back to get moving. "If we're not back by six, pack up and go home, folks."

The time was three-thirty.

"Are you kidding me? How long do you think this is going to take us?" Bob asked as they raced down the stairs.

"It depends on how long it's going to take us to get there and back. You know what the traffic can be like at this time of day."

"I suppose you're right. I never really thought about it. The traffic seems to be getting worse around Workington."

"Damn roadworks are a pain in the rear."

· · ·

WHEN SAM DREW UP, she found the surgery car park half-empty. "This seems promising. It shouldn't be too busy in there. I'm assuming most of these cars belong to the staff."

"Possibly. We'll soon find out."

Bob opened the door for Sam, and she muttered, "Creep," as she passed.

"Charming, and I thought I was being the perfect gentleman, for a change."

"You said it... for a change."

"You can go off people, you know, whether you're my boss or not."

Sam ignored him and approached the receptionist, who had looked up from her work when they entered. The waiting room was empty.

"Hello, can I help you?"

Sam produced her ID. "I'm Detective Inspector Sam Cobbs. Is it possible to speak to the person in charge? Would that be the practice manager?"

"Yes. Umm... Ruth is in with Doctor Hagan at the moment."

"Could I interrupt their meeting?" Sam pushed.

"Ah, I'm not sure. It depends on why you want to see her."

"It's regarding Doctor Morgan."

"Oh, I see. Let me check with them. Take a seat. I won't be long." The receptionist jogged up the short corridor and knocked on the nearest door. After an authoritative voice summoned her, she dipped her head into the room. She returned with an older, officious-looking woman in her fifties. "This is Ruth Webb, the practice manager." The receptionist went back to her post but kept an ear open on what was being said.

Sam showed her ID and introduced herself and Bob. "Is there somewhere we can chat privately?"

"This is most unusual—to get a visit from the police. However, in the circumstances, please come with me to my office."

Sam and Bob followed her to a room off the reception area. She invited them to take a seat once she'd removed a pile of files from one of the chairs.

"Excuse the mess. Because of what's happened, I'm a little behind on my day-to-day paperwork."

Sam smiled to put her at ease, then admitted, "I know that feeling. Please, you seem on edge. We're not here to interrogate you."

Ruth shook out her arms. "May I ask why you are here then?"

"We have some bad news to share with you."

Ruth's hands immediately slapped her cheeks. "No, please don't tell me Robert is dead?"

Sam gave a brief nod. "I'm sorry, he is."

"Shit! We were hoping this was all a mistake, that he'd taken himself off somewhere to clear his head, and now you're telling me he's not coming back. Oh God. I can't believe this. Does Melinda know? Of course she does. You wouldn't tell us before you'd broken the news to her, would you? Oh, that poor woman. I bet she's beside herself. I need to give her a call to see if we can do anything to help her."

"In time. I'd leave it for today. She's coping. I don't think the news had fully sunk in by the time we left her. It would be nice if you contacted her tomorrow, just to let her know that you're thinking about her."

"I'll do that," Ruth replied, her voice quaking a touch. "I never thought it would come to this. Sorry, it's come as a bit of a shock to me. I'm not sure if I'm going to be of much use to you."

"It's okay, take your time. We realise how difficult this must be for everyone who knew him. However, in order for us to move the investigation forward, we need to try to understand how Doctor Morgan was murdered and, more importantly, why."

"I understand that, but I'm not sure if I can tell you anything. Yes, we worked together. Other than that, I didn't really know him. He preferred to keep himself to himself. He wasn't the type to join us when we arranged an evening out, not like the other doctors at the surgery."

"That matches what his wife told us," Sam said, choosing her words carefully. Although she trusted what Doreen had confided in her, she still needed to get an all-round picture of what Morgan was like from the people who had known him best, his colleagues. "What was he like to work with?"

Ruth fidgeted in her chair, then looked Sam in the eye and said, "Putting it simply, there were days when I got the impression he didn't want to be here. He could be stubborn, I suppose, more difficult to work with than the other doctors at the surgery."

"I see. How did that translate when he dealt with his patients?" Sam had a rough idea by what Doreen had told her, but her aim was to see if Ruth would confide in her.

Ruth glanced around the room and heaved out a sigh. "Oh God, I hope I'm not struck down for saying this, especially now that Robert is dead... he wasn't the best. Excuse the pun, but sometimes his patience when dealing with the patients left a lot to be desired. It could be awkward some days. I've been out there, filling in for Lucy on reception, when he's sent a patient off without appearing to have listened to them. A couple of them have raised concerns about his lack of empathy in the past."

"A couple of them? Have those concerns ever turned into a complaint?"

"That's where I come in. It's my job to ensure that never happens. I've had to move some of the patients off Robert's list to one of the other doctors without him realising it. It's a balancing act, being a practice manager. It's my duty to ensure everyone is happy... although, saying that, Robert was a tough character to keep happy most days." Her gaze dropped to her clenched hands. "I'm sorry if that came across as being disrespectful; I didn't mean it to be."

"It didn't. Thank you for being honest with us. Did his attitude towards his patients raise any other concerns for you? By that, I mean, did any of the patients, or possibly a family member of theirs, come to the surgery and make any threats towards him?"

"God, no. Heaven forbid that should happen. He really was a law unto himself. I think his demeanour has changed severely over the last few years. I did my best to try to speak to him about it, but the shutters always came down, and he refused to open up to me. Even Doctor Hagan tried to find out what was going on with him, but he ended up telling her to bugger off. She found it upsetting at the time and backed off. Her attitude towards him changed after that encounter."

"Are you telling us that there was an atmosphere here at the surgery?" Sam pushed, intrigued to learn more.

Ruth shook her head and then, after a few seconds, nodded. "I suppose there must have been, even though I refused to believe it was possible. I don't know about you, Inspector, but if there's a bad penny within the ranks, it can make life awkward for everyone within a workplace."

"Absolutely, and it was your job to keep the peace at all times, right?"

"I tried. It didn't always work out that way. Let's just say I'm glad there aren't a lot of employees here."

Sam smiled. "Maybe things will return to normal for you."

Ruth's eyes widened. "I suppose they will, not that I would have wanted this outcome to solve the issue. I think his heart was in the right place, maybe some of the time. At Christmas, he always gave a large donation to the charity the surgery chose to raise money for, so he couldn't have been all bad."

"That's good to hear. Has there ever been any trouble here at the surgery because of his off-hand approach to people?"

"No, not really. Most of the patients just accepted him for the way he was. He's not the only doctor I've dealt with over the years who was a bit off with his patients, but I'd say he didn't hold back from showing his intolerance to the patients, if that makes sense?"

"It does. Tell me, did he ever confide in you or any of the other members of staff?"

"Confide in us? Regarding what?"

Sam shrugged. "Anything. What was going on with his personal life. If he had any issues, either personally or professionally, that were taking their toll on him, perhaps?"

"No, definitely not. As I said earlier, he generally kept himself to himself. Sometimes we'd meet up outside of work, you know, go for a meal or the theatre as a group, and although we made a concerted effort to invite him, he always declined. He made every excuse under the sun as to why he couldn't attend, even if we tried to work around him or change the dates for the outing. He often got nasty if we pushed him too hard. In the end, we stopped inviting him, which was a shame because I felt it put a wedge between us. Maybe it did, and maybe it didn't. It might have just felt that way sometimes."

"I understand. Do you think all was well at home with his wife?"

"I think so, but who can tell these days? Maybe he was having an affair, and that's why he didn't want to meet up with us. But then again, I might be talking crap. It's probably the latter, if I'm honest with you."

"Do you know Melinda very well?"

"I used to. I'd say she's distanced herself from the surgery in recent years. Again, I'm not privy as to why that would be."

"That's interesting to know, thank you. Is there anything else you can tell me that you might have found odd about Doctor Morgan in recent months?"

"No, not really, other than his anger mounting at times at the merest hint of things going wrong."

"As in, his patience snapping?"

"Yes, that's exactly how I would put it."

"Okay, as the surgery doesn't appear to be busy right now, would it be possible to speak with the other members of staff, including the other doctors?"

"We might not appear busy to you, but at this time of day, the other doctors are in their offices, calling patients or doing the necessary paperwork to keep the practice going."

"I appreciate that. We're prepared to wait until they have some spare time, maybe between patients."

"I'll need to check with them to see how busy Doctor Hagan and Doctor Attle are this afternoon. As for the other members of staff, there's only Lucy, who you met at reception. I can take over from her for ten minutes if you want a quick chat with her next. That'll give me time to assess the doctors' diaries."

"That would be great. Thanks."

"You can use my office. I'll ask Lucy to come in and see you. Would you like a drink?"

"No, don't worry, we're fine, thanks."

Ruth left the room.

"Huh, speak for yourself. My mouth is drier than sandpaper right now," Bob complained.

Sam rolled her eyes. "Maybe we can ask Lucy to make you one after we've spoken with her. How's that?"

"Better. You need to look after your staff or they're likely to go on strike. Just saying."

"Poppycock. You do talk a lot of twaddle when you're pushed into a corner."

Their conversation was interrupted by a quiet knock on the door.

Sam jumped out of her seat to answer it. "Hi, Lucy. Don't be shy, come in."

"Umm... Ruth said that you wanted to have a chat with me."

"That's correct. Take a seat."

"In Ruth's chair?"

Sam smiled and nodded. "Why not?"

"Have I done something wrong? I've never had a reason to have a chat with the police before, either at work or outside."

Sam raised a hand. "Please, there's no need for you to be concerned. All we're doing is making general enquiries. We're hoping you can help us with our investigation."

"Investigation? Into what?"

"I take it Ruth hasn't told you why we're here today?"

"No, she's told me nothing. That's why I'm bricking it, sorry, why I'm worried about seeing you."

"Please don't be. You've done nothing wrong. Are you aware that Doctor Morgan went missing two days ago?"

"Yes. Ruth and I have been rearranging his appointments in his absence. It's unlike him to go off the radar without telling either of us where he's going or when he'll be back."

"Unfortunately, we have some bad news to share with you."

Lucy frowned and sat forward. "What's that? Has he been

arrested? I know his car was found damaged. Don't tell me he had an accident and didn't report it?"

"No, it's nothing like that. Doctor Morgan was found dead this morning."

"What? No, you must be wrong. He can't be dead. How? Was he hurt during the accident? We wondered where he had got to. Did someone take him to the hospital? I rang all of them in the area to see if he had been admitted, but they couldn't tell me anything. Was he dazed and confused?"

Sam struggled to keep up with all the questions Lucy was firing at her. "Let's get one thing straight: there is no suggestion that he died because of the accident."

"I don't understand. What are you saying, then?"

"That he was murdered."

Lucy slapped a hand over her mouth and fell back in her seat. The executive chair dwarfed her slight frame. "No, he can't have been murdered, not Robert."

The way she uttered her boss's name caused Sam to question their relationship. "How well did you know him?"

Lucy sat upright, and her cheeks coloured up. "He was a colleague." She wagged a finger. "No, don't even suggest that we were more than that. God, the thought of it. I'm not that type of girl. For a start, he's a married man, and I've got a steady boyfriend. Nothing could be further from the truth, I assure you. I'm just shocked because someone I know has been murdered. That's never happened to me before. How am I supposed to react to the news? You probably deal with these types of crimes on a weekly or daily basis. I don't. This is a first for me. I swear, there's nothing more to it than that. Do you know who killed him or why?"

"Not yet. Our investigation is still in the preliminary stages; hence, we have come here today to see what you and your colleagues can tell us about him."

"Wow. Who'd have thought it? I know he could be a bit mardy at times, but for someone to go after him and kill him, well, that's below the belt, isn't it? I take it that's what has happened?"

"We don't know. Any idea why his body was found at the abandoned clinic in Workington?"

"Me? How would I know? Hey, you don't think I had anything to do with this, do you? First of all, you sit there accusing me of knowing him better, and then you're asking me why his body was found at the clinic. This is all news to me. You're going to have to take my word for it. Christ, if you dig hard enough, I bet you come up with a bucketload of people who'd like nothing more than to bump him off."

Sam cocked an eyebrow. "Really? Care to give us some idea of who you might be talking about?"

"There you go again, reading something into it—not that I meant anything by it. No doubt you're aware of his reputation by now, after speaking to Ruth."

"We are. How did you get on with him?"

"Hard to say, really. I suppose you'd call it an ultra-professional relationship. I knew where I stood with him. He made that clear the second I joined the surgery."

"When was that?"

"Eighteen months ago. The other two doctors are more relaxed. I can have a laugh with them. Everyone knew they had to be on their best behaviour with Robert, though. I tried to play a trick on him once. I put salt in his coffee instead of sugar as an April Fool's prank. He went ballistic and told me I was a juvenile little girl who should know better. Actually, he issued me with a written warning. I was in tears and threatened to walk out. Doctor Hagan stepped in. She spoke up for me and forced Robert to back down. He withdrew the warning and mumbled a half-hearted apology. From that day, I was always wary of him."

"Wary that he would carry out his threat and issue another warning?"

"Yes. It's always good to keep your guard up with some people. My mum told me that when I started applying for jobs after I'd left sixth form. I thought she was winding me up to be honest with you. That was until I felt the mighty wrath of Robert Morgan."

"Sorry you had to go through that. We've heard from Ruth that he'd had several complaints against him. Can you tell us more about those?"

"No, it's none of my business. Ruth needs to tell you about those."

Which she had. This was Sam trying to find out if Ruth could be trusted. "No problem. Can you tell us if you've ever seen Doctor Morgan get into any spats or fights with anyone, either at the surgery or perhaps in an altercation outside, in the car park?"

"No, I haven't. You think someone killed him because of a fight or because they'd had a disagreement with him?"

"I don't know. It just seems a logical question for me to ask." Sam inhaled a large breath, disappointed at the outcome of the interviews so far. "What about his wife, Melinda? Do you know anything about her?"

"No, not really. I think I've only spoken to her once or twice over the phone and only seen her once when she popped in to visit Robert. I seem to recall it was some kind of an emergency. I never really found out what it was about. He was very secretive in that respect."

"Thanks. Okay, if you can't tell us anything else, you're free to go back to work."

"Phew, thanks. It wasn't as bad as I thought it was going to be. When will you find out who has killed him?"

Sam smiled. "How long is that proverbial piece of string we all go on about? There's no time limit on these things. It's usually dependent on what information comes our way. As it is, we've got very little to go on—only that he was a grumpy doctor who tended to keep himself to himself."

Lucy pointed at Sam. "I'd say that sums him up perfectly. Sorry I haven't been much help. I hope some useful information comes your way soon. It must be awful for Melinda, going through what she's dealing with right now."

"It's never easy for the relatives who are left behind."

"I can only imagine what nightmares she's going to have to deal with."

Lucy left the room. "What do you make of that?" Bob asked. "She seemed a touch defensive to me."

"Yeah, you're not wrong. We'll bear it in mind, though I'm not sure I would go so far as to note her as a person of interest. I think she's probably just a snippy cow."

With that, Ruth entered the office.

"Hi, again. I've had a chat with Doctor Attle and Doctor Hagan, and they've both said they can fit you in within the next half an hour or so, if that's any good?"

"That would be brilliant. Thanks for accommodating us. The sooner we can interview everyone at the surgery, the quicker we can get on with the investigation."

"That's what I told them. They were both shocked to hear the news of Robert's passing. I hope I did the right thing in telling them. I needed to get across how important it was for you to speak with them today."

"That's fine. You did the right thing."

"What about a drink now, while you're waiting?"

"Thank you. Two coffees, both white, one with one sugar and the other with two."

"I think I can guess which is which. My husband has a sweet tooth, too." She chuckled and left the room.

"Who's the predictable one now?" Sam leaned in and whispered.

"Get a life. I've got a feeling our visit here today isn't going to amount to much."

Sam tutted and ran her tongue over her dry lips. "I was thinking the same thing. Doreen was right; he was a mardy bloody doctor."

"Yeah, sounds like he made the wrong career move, right?"

"Not half. I wonder if something had changed over the last few months to make him worse."

"I suppose only Mrs Morgan will be able to tell us that, if he was the secretive sort, and she never mentioned anything to us this morning. There seems to be more to this case than first meets the eye."

"Yeah, that's the frustrating part. We know there's something amiss, but it's finding a clue to lead us to that nugget of information —that's always the key factor that eludes us."

Sam stopped talking when Ruth entered the room with their drinks. "Here you are. Two sugars for you, Sergeant." Ruth handed Bob a mug decorated with sunflowers.

"Thanks. We really appreciate it. It's been a while since the boss has let me have a break to replenish my caffeine levels."

Ruth smiled. "She looks a hard taskmaster. And here's yours, Inspector. Doctor Attle should be free in ten minutes, just enough time for you to enjoy your drinks."

Sam reached for her plain mug and asked, "Wonderful. Thanks ever so much, Ruth. Is Lucy all right?"

Ruth frowned. "Why? Did she get upset?"

"A little to begin with. She couldn't really tell us much."

"Like all of us, I suspect." Ruth exited the room.

"We've seen it before, either the doc was neck-deep in debt after gambling on the sly, or he's done something in his past that has caught up with him," Bob said. He blew on his coffee and took a sip.

Sam paused to mull over his suggestion and then rang the station. "Claire, it's me. Have the financial reports for the victim come back yet?"

"Funny you should say that. I'm just going through them now."

"Anything untoward in there?"

"I haven't spotted anything so far. He's got over a hundred grand in a savings account and around three thousand in his current one."

"The hundred grand—is that down as a one-off payment, or has it been drip-fed into that account over the years?"

"The latter. Like I said, I haven't seen anything suspicious that has caught my attention so far."

"Hmm... okay, keep digging. Can you get one of the boys to check the archives and see if there has been any scandal written about him over the years, or if he has ever been caught up in anything that could be classed as damning to his reputation?"

"I'll get Nick on it. I take it the people at the surgery couldn't shed any light on anything."

"We've only spoken to the two members of staff. We're waiting to talk to the other two doctors. They're currently making video calls to some of their patients. So far, just like you, we've drawn a complete blank."

"We'll crack on with things at this end. Good luck."

"Thanks. You too, Claire." Sam ended the call and took a sip from her mug. "I'm sensing this is going to be one of those cases that has 'frustrating for the investigation team' written all over it."

"Nothing new there then. What can we do to combat that?"

Sam shrugged. "I wish I knew. Feel free to throw some inspirational tips my way."

Bob grinned. "You'll be the first to know if I come up with anything."

Ruth entered the room again. "Doctor Attle is free now, if you'd like to see her."

"That would be great. In here?"

"She's asked if you can hold the meeting or interview in her office. It would be more convenient for her, as she has another call to make in fifteen minutes, and moving between the two rooms would take up too much of her time." Ruth bit her lip.

Sam wondered if that decision had been Ruth's and not the doctor's. She took another sip from her mug and got to her feet. "That's fine by us. Are you ready, Sergeant?"

Bob downed the rest of his coffee and scrambled out of his seat. He wiped his mouth on the back of his hand. "I'm good to go."

Ruth led them past the reception desk. Lucy glanced up and gave an awkward smile, then returned to her work. Ruth introduced Sam and Bob to Doctor Gail Attle, who invited them to take a seat. Her eye make-up was slightly smudged, as if she'd been crying.

Sam sat opposite her and said, "Thank you for agreeing to see us, Doctor. We realise how busy the surgery is."

"Has Ruth told you how much time I have before my next appointment?"

"Yes, she's made it perfectly clear."

"I'll leave you to it," Ruth said and exited the room.

"I have to tell you from the outset how shocked I was to hear the news. Robert wasn't the easiest person to get along with. He could be stubborn and downright rude most of the time, but that doesn't excuse someone choosing to kill him. It's so wrong. The world is made up of all sorts of different people, both good and bad. Is that any reason to take someone's life?"

"Right now, we haven't got a single idea why anyone would want to end his life the way they did. Our job is to find out more about his character and see if any of his colleagues can give us an indication as to why his life was ended."

"You're not accusing us of having something to do with his death, are you?"

"No, that's not what I was suggesting at all. I'm guessing you would have spent more time working alongside him than the average friend or relative, such as his wife. Therefore, it would make sense that if anything had happened to spark someone's anger towards Doctor Morgan, it would have taken place here, at the surgery."

"Well, if it did, I wasn't aware of it. Ruth mentioned that he was found at the abandoned clinic in town. That news has baffled me. Why would he go there?"

"I don't think it was his idea. We believe he was abducted, maybe kept there against his will for the two days he was missing, and then... killed."

"Oh crap! That's not something I had even considered. That poor man. Hold on, are you saying that he was tortured before he died?"

"We're awaiting the pathologist's report to verify how he died. What we know at present, and I'm only telling you this because you're a doctor, is that his heart was removed."

"Jesus. Why? Who would stoop to such a low level? It doesn't matter how rude or offensive he was; he didn't deserve to die at the hands of another person."

"You're right, no one does. We asked Ruth and Lucy if Doctor Morgan had fallen out with anyone at the surgery. They didn't divulge any names, but I think he'd had several run-ins with patients over the years, hadn't he?"

"That's true. Ruth did her best to step in and prevent the situation from escalating by switching those patients to either Helen or me. Most of it was done on the quiet rather than set Robert off. However, there's no way any of those patients would have sought revenge; at least, I don't think they would have."

"When was the last time a patient was transferred to either you or Doctor Hagan?" Sam asked.

Doctor Attle considered the question for a few moments, then replied, "Hard to say without checking the system." She turned to her computer and brought up a file. "Ah, yes. Mr Winchell came over to me nearly a year ago. Surely that would be regarded as too long ago, wouldn't it?"

Sam sighed. "Yes, you're right. We're looking for something that might have taken place within the last couple of months."

She tapped her keyboard and shook her head. "No, I can't see anything of note on the system. The last patient who switched to Helen was over six months ago; that was Mrs Cooper."

"Not to worry. Thanks for your help."

"It's the least I can do. Is Melinda all right?"

"She was coping when we last saw her. Obviously, the news came as a shock to her. She'd been expecting him to return, just like you had. Do you all leave the premises at the same time at the end of the day?"

"Mostly. Why?"

"I wondered if Robert might have been ambushed in the car park, maybe after his shift?"

"Ambushed? By a disgruntled patient?"

"Yes, or possibly someone working at one of the neighbouring premises whom he might have had a run-in with."

"Nothing like that has ever happened around here. We have a large enough car park not to affect the other business owners in the vicinity. I really do think you're barking up the wrong tree, Inspector."

"I see. Okay, maybe he dropped his guard with you occasionally and revealed what was going on in his personal life?"

Doctor Attle shook her head. "Sorry, it never came to that. We didn't have any real personal chats. I'm sure the others will back me up on that count, too. He was a closed book to everyone. I honestly wish there was something that I could think of that might help you with your investigation. The truth is, there isn't."

"Not to worry, it was worth a shot. Would it be all right if we still spoke with Doctor Hagan?"

"Of course. She might come up with something to assist you. I'm sorry to have let you down."

"You haven't. Thank you for talking to us. We'll leave you to get on with your appointments."

"If you go back to the reception area, Ruth will tell you when Doctor Hagan has a free slot available to see you."

"Thanks."

Sam and Bob left the office.

"Another waste of time," her partner grumbled on their way back.

"Keep the faith, Bob. I'm sure something will come our way soon. It has to."

"And if it doesn't?"

Sam sighed. "I haven't thought about that. Doctor Hagan is our last hope, for now."

"How did you get on?" Ruth asked as soon as she saw them.

"No good. We're going to be reliant on what Doctor Hagan can tell us now. Any idea how long she's going to be?"

Ruth consulted the list on her clipboard. "I'm afraid she won't be free for another ten minutes or thereabouts."

"Don't worry. Can we sit here in the waiting room?"

"Feel free. I'll let Doctor Hagan know that you're waiting to speak with her."

Sam smiled, and Ruth walked away from them. Sam stifled a yawn and closed her eyes for a few seconds.

Bob nudged her. "Hey, don't you go falling asleep on me."

She faced him and winked. "Would I do that?"

"It has been known."

"Piss off," she whispered.

Lucy must have heard her because she glanced up and laughed.

"Sorry," Sam apologised.

"There's no need. I can imagine how stressful your job must be. It's good to have a bit of banter. It can often brighten one's day."

"It doesn't happen that often, but yes, sometimes it's called for to ease the tension during our day."

Ruth returned. "Doctor Hagan finished her appointment early and said she'll see you now."

Sam and Bob leapt out of their chairs, eager to complete the interview and get back to the station.

"That's great news."

Ruth knocked on the furthest door and introduced them to the female doctor. She was in her early forties, had shoulder-length brown hair and was wearing a smart black jacket. Sam assumed that it belonged to either a skirt or trouser suit, but it was hard to tell with the woman still sitting.

"Thank you for agreeing to see us," Sam began. "We shouldn't take up much of your time."

Ruth backed out of the room and closed the door behind her.

"To say I was shocked to learn of Robert's death would be an understatement. Do you know why or how he was killed?"

"All we can tell you at this preliminary stage is the how. He was murdered. We believe the killer abducted him after the accident he had two days ago. His body was found in the abandoned clinic in town."

"Yes, Ruth told me that. What can I do to help?"

"We've come to ask if you, or any of the other staff, could tell us whether Robert has been in any trouble lately, possibly with a patient, or if he'd had a dispute with one of the other business owners in the area."

Doctor Hagan stared at the wall behind Sam, and after a moment or two, shook her head. "I'm sorry, no, I can't think of anything."

"Did you get on with Robert?"

"As well as anyone else did at the surgery. He was a strange man, to say the least. He didn't mingle well and pretty much kept himself to himself."

"That's what the others told us. Did he open up to you about his home life at all?"

"Not really. He just wasn't the type. I'm sorry, I'm not trying to be awkward or anything. I suppose the best way to describe him is to say he was angry most of the time and definitely not a team player. To tell you the truth, it frustrated the hell out of Gail and me. We tried our hardest to involve him in activities outside surgery hours, but he didn't want to know."

"Okay. I'll leave you one of my cards. If anything should come to mind after we've left, could I ask you or one of the others to give me a call? It would really help our investigation because, quite frankly, we've got little to nothing to go on right now."

"I'm sorry. No doubt we'll have a discussion about it after you leave. I promise you we'll get in touch if anything comes to mind."

"Thank you. Sorry to have disrupted your afternoon."

"You haven't, not really. Let's hope you find the person responsible for Robert's murder soon."

Sam and Bob left the surgery. When they returned to the car, Sam noted the time on the dashboard—it was just after five. She sat there for a while without starting the engine.

"Are you all right? Do you want to share what's going through that complex mind of yours?" Bob asked.

"I'm thinking. This car park is quite open. We know that Robert made a home visit to a patient the night of the accident. What if the killer was sitting in his vehicle, watching and waiting for him to leave work?"

"I'd say that was a given. Ah, I'm getting where this is going now." He pointed at the small camera on the surgery wall. "Do you want me to go back inside?"

"Wait, I'm struggling to comprehend why the four members of staff haven't mentioned the camera during the interviews."

"It does seem odd, unless the damn thing is for show or isn't functioning properly."

"Maybe. Go on then, go ask the question."

Bob grumbled and left the car.

Sam took the opportunity to call Rhys. "Hi, have you finished for the day?"

"Yes, are you and Tilly back home now?"

"Tilly is. I was called into work a few hours ago. I drove back and dropped Tilly off at Doreen's."

Rhys let out a long sigh. "Sam, I thought you said you needed to take time out for a few hours."

"I did that. It's a murder investigation. I had to come in. Anyway, that's not why I'm calling. I wondered what your plans were for dinner this evening. Have you got any?"

"I haven't, not really. I don't fancy cooking, do you?"

"My thoughts exactly. Someone mentioned they had a fabulous meal at The Royal Yew at Dean. I wondered if you were up for it. It's a dog-friendly pub, so we can take Casper and Tilly with us."

"That sounds great. It's a date, then, for all of us."

"Fantastic. I'll book a table when I get five minutes."

"Leave it for me to do. I haven't got anything on. In fact, I was just packing up to go home. Do you want me to take the dogs for a walk when I get back or leave it until we go out later?"

"It might be a good idea to take them just in case we can't find a suitable walk out that way later."

"Gotcha. What time shall I book a table for?"

"Seven-thirty? It's been a while since we've been out during the week."

"I'll give them a call now. Looking forward to it. Love you, Sam."

"Love you, too," she said as Bob returned to his seat.

"Aww... thanks. I wasn't gone that long."

She slapped her partner's thigh for being such an idiot. "I was talking to Rhys."

He smiled and waved a disc at her. "I knew that. I've got the footage from his final day at work. Ruth apologised for not mentioning it and blamed the shock of hearing the news."

"It's fine. I can understand how upset they must have all been. I don't think it was intentionally missed."

"Me neither."

Sam drove back to the station. The first thing they did when they arrived was to view the footage with the rest of the team. However, none of them saw anything that could be deemed as suspicious on the disc.

Sam pressed the Off switch, and the TV went blank. "That just about sums this case up so far. We keep drawing nothing but blanks. Have you guys found anything while we've been out and about?"

Disappointingly, the team all shook their heads. "Right, then I suggest we call it a day and start afresh in the morning."

The team agreed and began switching off their computers, everyone except Claire. Sam walked towards her. "You've been exceptionally quiet since we got back. Is everything okay, Claire?"

"I have a lot on my mind, boss. Would it be all right if I worked a little longer this evening? There's something that's bugging me, and I'd like to do some extra digging before I bring it to your attention."

"If that's what you'd prefer. You're going to make me feel guilty, going on a date night while you're slaving over a hot keyboard."

"Don't be daft. You go out and enjoy yourself. It's been ages since Scott and I went out, or so it seems."

"It's good for the soul to get out with our partners, especially during the week. Don't work too long. You can always crack on with the task in the morning. It's not like we have much else to deal with at the moment."

"I know. I should only be an hour at the most."

"Cool. Do you want to come in an hour later in the morning?"

"There's no need. I'll be here at my normal time."

Sam squeezed her shoulder and went into her office to ensure everything was switched off in there. She stopped by the window to admire the view. It was always spectacular at this time of the day. The sun's rays were beaming through the fluffy clouds. If she weren't trying to find a sadistic killer, the day would be perfect. Unfortunately, life never turned out to be that simple.

. . .

Forty minutes later, Sam drew up outside her cottage. Doreen was standing at the lounge window next door, waving. She knocked on the door, and Doreen came to open it.

"How are you doing?"

"I'm all right, Sam. I've been worried sick about you all afternoon, after the news you shared with me earlier. I can't get Morgan's death out of my mind. I don't suppose you've had any news yet, have you?"

"No, it's far too soon for that, Doreen. I hope Tilly didn't run you ragged this afternoon?"

"She didn't. We had a quick game of fetch in the back garden before she decided she'd rather have a nap instead. You must have worn her out this morning on your trip to Coniston. You've got yourself a very sweet dog there, love."

"I know. I hope she doesn't prove to be a handful for you to deal with over the coming months. I've been told it can take a rescue pup some time to settle into a family's routine."

"I'd say she's pretty much there already. I'll tell you if she's having a problem. I won't hold back, I promise. I'm glad you and Rhys are going out for a meal tonight. You both work far too hard and never seem to take time off to enjoy yourselves."

"Really? I wouldn't say that. We do okay at the weekends when we have time off. I'm never one to turn down the chance of free food. Oops, there's me presuming that he'll be paying the bill."

"He will because he's a true gent. Dare I ask how the wedding plans are coming along?"

"You're asking the wrong person. Apparently, Crystal has it all under control. All Rhys and I have to do is show up for the big day."

"I received my invite. Thank you. I'm worried about who is going to take care of the dogs, though, if we're all at the venue on the day."

"I've had a word with the hotel. They've told me Casper and Tilly can attend the reception."

"Wow, that'll be good, if they can come along, too. You'd better get yourself ready. Time is marching on, Sam. Thank you for dropping in to see me."

Sam kissed her on the cheek and hugged her. "You're welcome to join us for dinner, unless you've already eaten."

"You don't want me hanging around your neck like a spare part. Anyway, I've had my dinner earlier, but thank you for the offer."

"We should go there for Sunday lunch one day."

"Now that would be lovely. Let me know what the food is like when you drop Tilly off in the morning."

"I will. See you tomorrow, Doreen."

Rhys and the dogs were still out when she got home. She prepared the dogs' dinners and then ran upstairs to jump in the shower. When she came out of the bathroom, Rhys was standing in the bedroom.

"Blimey, you scared me half to death."

"Sorry. The dogs are eating. I managed to book the table. Are you getting dressed up for our date?"

"I wasn't intending to. I had to have a shower. I felt lousy because of the clinic we visited earlier this afternoon."

"I don't blame you. Is that where the body was found?"

"Yes. I'll tell you about it later."

He grimaced. "Not over dinner, I hope."

"Maybe we'll discuss it on the way home instead."

"Sounds like the perfect solution to me." He crossed the room to the wardrobe and removed a pair of khaki trousers and a cream short-sleeved shirt. "How about this ensemble?"

"Looks spot on to me. I was going to wear black trousers and a white shirt."

"You'd look good going out in that." He pointed at the towel wrapped around her slender body.

"Charmer."

The dogs thundered up the stairs and bounced into the bedroom. Tilly flung herself at Sam, expecting a cuddle, and then flopped on her back, wanting a belly rub.

"She's such an adorable girl."

"I had my doubts if she would slot in. I thought it might have been too soon after losing Sonny to welcome another dog into the fold, but she has proved me wrong. What's more, Casper loves her to bits."

"We're going to be the perfect family in a few weeks, husband and wife with two kids to care for. It's all I've ever wanted."

He shuffled his feet. "Umm... we've never really discussed the prospect of having children, have we?"

Here it comes, crunch time. After failing IVF five times with Chris, I haven't really considered going through all that with someone else.

"We will, one day. We'd better get a move on. It'll take me ten minutes or so to dry my hair and get ready."

"I can take the hint. I'll jump in the shower myself."

THEIR MEAL TURNED out to be one of the best Sam had eaten in a long time. She couldn't wait to treat Doreen to Sunday lunch and ended up booking a table for the three of them in a couple of weeks. "She's going to love it, and they do a smaller roast dinner, which will suit Doreen better."

"I can't believe we haven't been there before. It was sensational, and you're right, Doreen will love it. Right, now that the evening is over and the dogs have passed out on the back seat, you can tell me about your murder investigation."

Sam closed her eyes for a second or two. She opened them and faced him. "Do I have to? It might spoil our wonderful evening."

"Not if you don't feel like it."

In the end, she decided to open up to him.

"I'm in shock right now. How awful to lose your life like that after being a caring member of the community."

"That's debatable. I've had it on good authority from Doreen that his bedside manner was somewhat lacking at times."

"Do you think a patient killed him?"

Sam shrugged. "I don't have a clue. It's going to be difficult to find out who actually did the deed. We've viewed the CCTV footage from the surgery and didn't see anything out of the ordinary around the time he left work on the evening he went missing."

"I don't envy you. However, I have every confidence in your ability to figure it out. You always do."

"Not always. There are a few cases to my name that I've failed to close over the years, mainly up in Liverpool, but they still haunt me all the same."

"I learn something new about you every day."

"I prefer to keep you on your toes, Mr Wilkins."

His gaze left the road for a split second, and he grinned. "Oh, you do that all right."

3

Claire tapped at her keyboard, the glow of the screen casting her face in ghostly hues. The station was quiet. The clock on the wall ticked towards nine forty in the evening. She had worked far longer than she'd anticipated. The rest of the team had gone home hours ago, but she had volunteered to stay behind because she liked the solitude. It gave her space to think.

An email popped into her inbox.

SUBJECT: **You Missed Something**
From: Unknown

SHE FROWNED and reread the message a few times. The thing that surprised her more than anything was that it wasn't routed through the Force's secure channels. It had come from a basic email account —one that she had a feeling would prove to be untraceable.

The message was brief and to the point:

· · ·

You're smart, Claire. Smarter than most. That's why I picked you.

But during your research, you overlooked something important. Do you want answers?

Meet me at Whitehaven Harbour. 10:15 p.m. Come alone.

She stared at it, her heart pounding. Her instincts screamed that she was being set up, or that this could be a trap. But another part of her—the part that had been itching at something for the past few days—was hooked. *Sam is going to kill me for not contacting her, but the message told me to come alone.*

Her mind made up, she grabbed her coat and slipped out of the station unnoticed, since the reception area had long been empty.

The harbour was deserted, bathed in the dim glow of half-working streetlights and the occasional flicker from the nearby moored boats. The wind carried the scent of seaweed and salt.

Trepidation filled Claire as she crept along the water's edge, every nerve on high alert as she peered into the shadows.

Footsteps sounded on the concrete behind her.

She turned, her hand instinctively brushing her coat pocket in search of her phone. But it wasn't there. Then she realised she'd left it back at the station, charging on her desk.

It was too late to regret that decision now.

"I came," she called out, trying to sound confident, eager to see who was there. "You wanted to talk? Come out and show yourself."

Silence filled the air.

A flash of something metallic caught her eye. She stepped forward to satisfy her curiosity and bent down to pick up a USB stick, partially wrapped in electrical tape. She reached for it but stopped when a whispered voice said, "You were close. So very close."

She spun one hundred and eighty degrees, ready to confront the individual. A figure emerged from the shadows, hooded and gloved.

"You?"

The person didn't speak. Instead, they lunged towards her.

Claire put up a good fight. Years on the force had taught her to be quick. She dodged most of the assailant's blows, except the one that landed on the back of her head. It had been swift and heavy, with a sense of finality.

Feeling the wind knocked out of her, she slumped onto the slipway. Blood seeped into the cracks of the concrete beneath her, crimson in her blurred vision. A sinking sensation swept through her. She was incapacitated, unable to move or even fight back. The USB stick, taunting her, lay just out of her grasp.

The figure towered over her, then crouched beside her and whispered something menacingly in her ear, "You should have stayed behind that desk of yours. There's a reason DI Cobbs doesn't trust you out in the field."

The person laughed, then skulked away and disappeared into the darkness, leaving her wondering what her fate would be. Would she be discovered by a passerby? She doubted it. She hoped she'd still be alive in the morning, but the likelihood of that happening was slipping fast.

Either way, she suspected the tide would already have taken what little evidence her attacker might have left behind, making it impossible to find them. This was her all-important final thought as the darkness consumed her.

4

Sam's phone vibrated on the bedside table. Sleepily, she picked it up and stared at the screen. It was only ten past six, fifty minutes before her alarm was set to go off. She sat up and answered it. "DI Sam Cobbs. This better be good."

"Ah, sorry to trouble you at this time of the morning, ma'am. I thought you would want to hear the news right away."

"I'm listening. What news?"

"A body has been discovered in Whitehaven Harbour this morning."

Sam glanced at Rhys, who was still fast asleep, his breathing slow and steady. Rather than disturb him, she threw back the quilt and finished her call in the en suite. "A body? Is this linked to the case I'm working on?"

"Umm... it is... Er, I'm sorry to have to inform you that it's a member of your team."

"What? Are you sure?" Sam's first thought was that the woman at the control centre was talking about Bob. Her legs wobbled. She sat on the edge of the bath to hear the rest. "Is it my partner?"

"No, it's Claire Owen, ma'am."

"It can't be. Not Claire. Are you sure?"

"Yes. Her warrant card was found on her person when the officers turned up to assess the scene. The pathologist is on his way."

Sam's head swirled with all types of scenarios she'd rather not have to consider at this time of day.

"Ma'am, are you still with me?"

"Sorry, yes. I'm still here. I'll get dressed and attend the scene. Can you put in a call to Bob Jones and request that he joins me? Don't tell him who the victim is. I'll bring him up to date at the scene. It's going to hit him hard, and I don't want him to have an accident en route."

"I understand. Are you okay, ma'am?"

"I don't know. I'll have a cold shower and let you know afterwards. I can't believe this is happening. She was one of our best officers... I dread to think how the other team members will cope with this news. I'm not sure how I will either, once it sinks in. Shit! She was... one of my best officers," Sam repeated, her voice trailing off at the end.

"With a great reputation at the station. She'll be missed, ma'am."

"How? How did she die? Did she fall and hit her head?"

"It wasn't an accident. Her hands were bound. A gentleman out walking his dog found her floating in the water."

"Shit! It gets worse. Okay, don't tell me anything else. I'll be there within half an hour. Thanks for the call."

"You're welcome. Do you need anything else from me?"

"I don't think so." Sam ran the shower and adjusted the dial to drop the temperature.

"Very well. I'm sorry for your loss. Please drive carefully."

"I will. Thanks." Sam ended the call, stripped off her PJs and stepped beneath the cool water. The shock took her breath away. Tipping her head back, she let the water pound her face as the thoughts ran through her mind.

How could this happen? I left her at the station. Did she find something out? Decide not to call me? Think she could handle the situation on her own?

She opened her eyes and slammed a fist into the wall, cracking one of the tiles in the process. She stared as the blood from the cut mixed with the water and surrounded her feet. Tears ran down her cheeks.

No, there has to be some kind of mistake. This can't be true. Not Claire! She was such a loyal officer...

Sam wrapped a flannel around her wound and stepped out of the shower. She waited a few seconds for the blood to wash away before she turned off the water. She stood there, hair dripping, some of it clinging to her face, staring at her reflection.

How could this be happening? Not Claire. Did she uncover something vital that led her to the killer?

All of this was pure speculation for now. She had to get to the location and see for herself. Sam wrapped a towel around herself, dried her hair with another towel and entered the bedroom to find Rhys getting out of bed.

He stretched and yawned. "You're up early." He rubbed a hand over his stomach. "I'm still full from last night. Can I make you some breakfast before you go? Wait, have you been crying?" He crossed the room to hug her. "Sam, are you all right? Tell me what's going on. It's not your father, is it?"

"No. I need to sit down."

He gripped her by the elbow and guided her to the bed. "You're worrying me. What is it? What's wrong, Sam?"

"I'm sorry. I didn't mean to worry you. I'm in shock. I thought I'd be okay after I had a cold shower. The truth is, I'm not."

"It's all right. Tell me in your own time. I'm going to make us a coffee. Stay there." He sprinted out of the bedroom, and the two dogs bounded down the stairs after him.

Sam stared at the doorway long after they had departed.

I should get dressed, but I can't. I feel like I'm in limbo. I need to get a grip, shake myself out of this. Otherwise, I'm going to be worse than useless at the crime scene.

She shook out her arms and summoned up the energy to sort out her outfit for the day. She chose a black trouser suit as a sign of respect for her dearly departed colleague.

Gone too soon, long before her time. She had so many adventures left ahead of her... Shit! I've got to break the news to Scott. That's going to be tough. He's an odd one; even though Claire loved him, there were still days when she struggled to handle him. He has a mind of his own and is one of those men who think they're always right, even when it's obvious they're wrong. I remember Claire telling me how he always needed to have the final word when they had an argument. It's not going to be easy... telling him that she's no longer with us.

Rhys entered the bedroom carrying two mugs. He placed one on the dressing table in front of her.

She raised her head and managed to offer up a slight smile of appreciation. "I'm sorry. You must think I'm a right idiot."

"Why? Something has obviously happened that has rocked your world. I'm not going to force you to tell me what that is. Just know that I'm here for you, ready to listen when you want to offload."

"Thanks, Rhys. I love you for being you."

He smiled. "That's good, because I have no intention of changing. You're stuck with me as I am."

"It's Claire, a member of my team... she's dead."

He walked back towards the bed, mug in hand. He sat on the corner. "What? Do you know how it happened? Was it an accident?"

"No. I don't know much about the incident, not yet. I'll know more when I turn up at the scene. I feel numb. She volunteered to stay behind after we all left the station last night. She told me she wanted to carry out some extra research on something before she presented it to me, presumably as evidence."

"Damn. Do you think she followed up a lead she found on someone, and they ended up killing her?"

"You tell me. That seems to be the most logical explanation. Oh God, I'm struggling to get my head around this one, Rhys. Why Claire?"

"You won't know that until you find the killer."

The dogs came running up the stairs again and separated when they entered the room. Little Tilly ran towards Sam, expecting her usual hug and tummy rub, but Sam didn't have it in her to give her one. Her mind was elsewhere.

"Sam. Love, please don't ignore her," Rhys prompted gently.

Tears filled her eyes, and she bent down to scoop Tilly into her arms. "I'm so sorry, sweetheart. Please forgive me." She sobbed into her pup's fur.

Rhys came towards her and rubbed Sam's back. "I'm sorry you're going through this. I know it's too raw to talk about right now, but please know that I'm here if you ever need to unload."

Tears blurred her vision as she looked up at him. "I'm sorry. I'm not sure what has come over me. I should be there at the scene. I just can't bring myself to go there... to face the truth that I've lost one of my officers."

"Do you want me to drive you? I think you should be there, but no one is going to blame you if you can't handle it, love."

She kissed the top of Tilly's head and put her on the floor. "Hug time over, sweetie. Mummy needs to get her shit together." She held out a hand to Rhys. He slipped his into hers. "Thank you for caring."

"Always. Sam, you're never alone, not with me around."

"Thank you. That means the world to me. I need to get my act together and get over there."

"The offer is still on the table if you want me to drive you."

"No, what you can do is take care of the dogs' needs for me. It's too early to drop Tilly off at Doreen's before I head off."

"Leave it with me. I'll see to the dogs."

"Thanks. You're the best fiancé anyone could hope to have."

He smiled, pulled her to her feet and gave her a tight hug. "Don't ever push me away. We're in this together, through the highs and lows, darling."

"I know. The news just knocked me for six. I feel better now I've had a cry to get it out of my system."

"Always what the doctor orders, venting those pent-up emotions. They can do the average person more harm than good."

Her eyes widened. "Nice to know where I stand, being called average in your eyes."

He cringed and shook his head. "Bugger, you know I didn't mean it like that. Stop twisting my words."

"I know. I'm just teasing." She continued to dry her hair, then slipped into her suit, teaming it with a red blouse. But she had second thoughts and swapped it for a cream one instead.

BOB WAS THERE to greet her at the scene. He marched towards her, waving his arms around. She prepared herself for an ear-bashing.

"Can you effing believe this? Shit! What the fuck is going on here? Did you know it was Claire?"

Sam raised her hands to silence him. "First of all, good morning. Can we hold fire on asking questions neither of us knows the answer to, for now at least? Yes, I knew. I told the girl at the call centre not to tell you. I didn't want you to have a crash en route. I need to see her."

"Sorry, morning. What a shitty way to start our day. She's over here."

"I thought Des would have been here by now. Have you heard from him?"

Before Bob could answer, Des's van appeared at the end of the harbour. The officer in charge checked the pathologist's credentials and then allowed him access to the harbour.

"I need to have a word with him."

"Shouldn't you see... Claire, first?"

Sam released a long sigh. "It's one of those cases where I want to, but at the same time, I don't. I'm aware that the images will haunt me for the rest of my life."

"I think you need time alone with her before you hand the scene over to Des. That's just my opinion. But what do I know?"

"Okay, you win. Let me get my protective suit on. How long have you been here?"

"Around ten minutes. I thought it would take you longer than normal to get here."

"It has. I had a hard time digesting the information when I was told this morning. That's why I requested you to attend the scene."

"What are you saying? That I'd deal with it better because I'm more in control of my emotions?"

"Yes, that's the case for most men, isn't it? God, I'm dreading telling the rest of the team, especially Nick, who has only just joined us."

"I wouldn't stress about it. I think you've got a much tougher task on your hands."

She stared at him and nodded. "Telling Scott?"

"Yeah. Good luck. I wouldn't want to be in your shoes."

"Right, let's see what we're up against. Was there any evidence found at the scene?"

"She was fished out of the harbour, so that's unlikely."

"Bugger. Who found her?"

Bob gestured to an elderly man with a border terrier standing at the end of the harbour wall. "Mr Torrence. He told me he didn't mind waiting around for a little while."

"In other words, he has a bird's-eye view of what's going on standing there and would prefer it if we left him alone to watch for a while."

"I think you've scored a hole in one there. Who could blame him? He's probably retired, and nothing interesting happens to brighten his day."

"I'll have a chat with him soon." Sam spotted Claire's body, hidden by the obligatory white sheet. She walked towards it, her legs heavy.

Bob bent and lifted the cover. Sam stared at the sergeant's face, with whom she'd had the pleasure of working for the past ten years or so.

"Oh, God. I hate seeing her like this. It's never easy dealing with a corpse, and it's even more difficult when that person is a serving police officer and a member of your team."

"What was she doing here? Did you know about this?" Bob mumbled.

"No. She told me she was researching something before sharing the details with me. Did she have a secret assignation with someone? Was it personal? I can't see it. So, this has to be connected to the case we're working. Did she discover something that triggered the killer, making them believe she was onto them? Did they tell her to meet them here, then kill her to silence her?"

"Too many questions and not enough answers, as usual. I guess we're going to learn more about that when we get to the station. You'd think there would be some form of trail left behind on her computer."

"We'll get it forensically analysed after we've had a quick look at it first."

Bob winked at her. "That's what I was thinking. You can't see it, but her hands have been bound with a cable tie."

"Makes me wonder if she was already dead, or if the killer wanted her to struggle before she took her last breath."

"We're going to need Des to give us more information about that."

"About what?" Des asked from behind Sam.

"If she was dead before she hit the water. Her hands are tied," Sam told him.

"I doubt if she was dead then. That's usually the way it works with these sadistic bastards. I've been told she's one of yours, Sam. I'm sorry for your loss."

"Believe me, so am I, Des. She was a great officer. I hope her death isn't in vain."

Des tilted his head and asked, "What do you mean by that?"

"Bob and I believe she found something out about the killer and... well, it's a shot in the dark at the moment, but we think she might have arranged to meet the killer at this location."

"How foolish of her. Why meet them alone? Was she hoping for a courage or bravery award?"

"She wasn't the type. Honestly, we don't know how or why this has happened. What we do know is that one of the most dedicated officers at the station has just lost her life."

"Is this a matter of concern for you, Sam? Should another team deal with this now?"

"I'll have a word with the DCI when I get back to the station. I'll request that we continue working the case, but I fear it will be stripped from us now, in light of Claire being murdered." She turned her back on the corpse and surveyed the area around them. "Bob, we need to source all the camera footage in the vicinity. I can see one or two on the shop frontages. Although they might be too far away, we still need to get them analysed."

"I'll get on it as soon as they open. It's still only seven-fifteen, Sam."

"Sorry, yes, you're right. I'll see what Mr Torrence has to say for himself and then send him on his way." She walked towards the elderly man. His dog barked at her.

"Hush now, Rex. Do you want to get us in trouble for disturbing the peace?"

"It's not a problem. I'm Detective Inspector Sam Cobbs, Mr Torrence. First of all, I'm so sorry it was you who discovered the body. Can you tell me what time that was?"

"Around five forty-five. I don't sleep well these days, so when the weather is fine, I like to take Rex for an early morning stroll around the harbour. I live in the block of flats around the corner. It's convenient for me, being this close to town. I don't drive now; let's face it, who can afford to run a car these days?" He came up for air and continued before Sam had a chance to ask another question. "Well, I came around the corner, and there it was, floating in the harbour. The state the water is in these days, that muddy orange colour, I knew it wouldn't be anyone daft enough to be having an early morning dip in there. When I got closer to the edge, I saw that the person was face down in the water. I immediately rang 999. The operator took my details and asked me to stay here until the patrol arrived."

Sam had jotted down all the information in her notebook as Bob was still busy talking to Des. "Thank you. You've given me a clear image of what happened. I don't suppose you saw anyone else in the area, did you?"

"I didn't. No, wait... I'm telling a lie. A man staying on board one of the boats came on deck. He saw me, and we had a brief chat. I pointed out the body. He hadn't noticed it; that's what he told me anyway."

"Which boat would that have been, sir?"

"The one with the flash of red on the side. I can't see the name of it from here."

"Not to worry. I'll have a word with him after I've finished talking to you."

"I thought you might. I would, too. You can't be too careful these days. He might pull up his anchor and set sail if you delay speaking to him."

"It's fine. I'll sort it. And you said you didn't see anyone else in the vicinity?"

"That's right. I didn't even see the little bugger who left the graffiti on the shop window over there." He pointed to the shop on the corner.

Sam withdrew her phone, took a picture and zoomed in on it due to her eyesight deteriorating lately. The message was written in red; it might have been blood, but without getting closer, Sam wasn't sure. It read, 'Traitor'.

What the heck? Was that directed at Claire? It must have been. It's too much of a coincidence otherwise.

"Forgive me for interrupting. You seem distracted. Do you know the victim?" he asked. "The reason I ask is because you seem upset. Or am I reading things into it?"

"You're very astute, Mr Torrence. She's a member of my team."

"A policewoman? Oh, no, I had no idea. Was she working a case?"

"Yes. I'm sorry. I can't go into detail."

"Of course. My wife Edna was always telling me that I'm a nosey git. God rest her soul. Despite our differences, I still miss her. She's been gone over ten years now. Rex is a comfort but not really the same. Forgive me, I'm waffling again. The police officer—was she married?"

"Yes. She also had two children. Around ten and twelve, I believe."

"How awful. Your lot really do put your lives on the line, don't you? I'm sure I speak for most of the community when I say this: we're grateful for the sacrifices you make to keep the public safe in the line of duty."

"Thank you. We really don't hear that enough from the public."

"Well, let's be honest, all the bad press the Met has received over the years probably puts all coppers in a bad light, I suppose."

"Yes, we've had to take the flack for that. Right, I'm going to need to get on now. If I can take your address, I'll get a uniformed officer to visit you at your convenience over the next few days to take a statement from you."

He gave her the relevant information and smiled. "It's just awful the young lady was killed. I sincerely hope you find the person who robbed her of her life. This type of thing shouldn't happen, not when all you're guilty of is doing your job."

"I agree. Unfortunately, it happens more than the public realises. Thank you for making the call this morning."

"Only doing my duty. I wish the outcome had been better for her and for you."

"Me too. Take care, Mr Torrence."

He smiled and jerked his dog's lead to get it to walk on. "Come on, Rex. Let's get home for some breakfast now, if we can stomach it."

Bob joined her as she watched the man and his dog walk back along the pier.

"There's something we've missed," Sam whispered.

"Huh? What's that?"

"Come with me."

They walked towards the row of shops.

"Shit. I can see it. What the fuck? Was that aimed at Claire?"

"I can only assume that it was. I hadn't noticed it when I drew up. The old man pointed it out to me."

Bob slammed his clenched fist against his thigh. "Why call her a traitor, and what secrets was she hiding?"

"I'm at a loss to know what this is about and if there's a connection to Morgan's murder. I'm trying to think back over the last couple of days as to how Claire had reacted to the news. Thinking about it, I suppose she's been quieter than normal. What do you think?"

"I can't really say. I hadn't noticed. I've been too wrapped up in the case. But if you think that, then it must be true."

Sam glanced over her shoulder at Claire's body and ran a hand around her face. "Not necessarily. Maybe it's me clutching at straws because there is nothing else for me to cling on to. Have you had a chance to look around yet? Do we know where she entered the water?"

Bob waved at a tech who was trying to get their attention on the slipway. "I was about to tell you that Paul has that in hand. I think our luck is in."

"What are we waiting for?"

They jogged over to the tech. "What have you found, mate?" Bob asked.

"Evidence of blood. Most of it has been washed away, presumably by the tide when it came in."

"Seems like a possible spot. Sam crouched for a closer inspection of the area. She saw the blood in the cracks, and tears misted her vision. "What did the bastard do to her?"

"We won't know that until Des has completed the PM," Bob admitted. "Hard to consider her being out here alone. What time did she get here? Why didn't she call one of us?"

"I'm probably to blame for her not doing that. I told her I was going out on a date night with Rhys."

"That's no excuse; she could have rung me. The fact is, she didn't. I know we don't want to consider the possibility of her being a bent copper, but the proof is mounting against her, Sam."

"I know," she reluctantly admitted. Sam was about to stand; however, something shiny caught her eye. She pointed at the object tucked away under a plank on the edge of the slipway. Not having any protective gloves on, she asked the tech, "Can you get that?"

He walked towards the plank and eased it aside. "It's a USB stick."

"What?" Sam rushed over to have a look for herself. "I wonder if Claire saw it before the person attacked her. Did the killer lead her to this specific spot? Tempt her with the idea of handing over the stick?"

"That's doesn't make sense," Bob said. "Why would the killer leave it here?"

"There's only one way to find out. We'll drop it over to the lab on our way back to the station."

"Let me bag it for you and make a note that you're taking it," Paul said.

"What's going on here?" Des joined them.

"We found a USB stick and clear signs of blood," Sam replied. "We're assuming that Claire was searching for the item and someone was watching her, possibly clobbering her over the head before she could retrieve the stick."

He nodded. "I've had a chance to quickly examine her body. I was coming over here to tell you that she has a gaping wound on the back of her head."

The rage built inside Sam. "So, what are we saying? That she was knocked out and then dumped into the harbour, left to drown in that filthy, disgusting water?"

"Possibly. I wouldn't like to commit to anything just yet," Des replied.

"I've seen enough. We're going to head off to the station. I need to see what she was working on last night. Something brought her to this location. It's nowhere near her home, so a walk after work to wind down wasn't on the agenda. We'll drop the USB stick off at the lab on our way."

"You do that. There should be someone there to assist you. If you want, I can give them a call and ask them to examine it while you're there."

"That would be great. I didn't want to suggest it in case your team are snowed under."

"We're always overworked, but I get the feeling the information on that thing might be essential to your investigation."

Sam laid her hand on his arm. "Thank you. From the bottom of my heart."

"You're welcome. I don't do sentimental offerings, so get out of here."

. . .

FIFTEEN MINUTES LATER, Bob drew up behind her in the lab car park. They entered the building together, and the tech, who was there to welcome them, invited them into his office.

"Right, let's see what we have for you," Mick said.

Sam and Bob remained silent and watched him work. He downloaded the information onto a file on the computer.

"Sorry for being a novice at all of this, but that seemed too easy, or did you just make it seem that way?" Sam asked.

Mick smiled. "I could tell you it was my expertise, but I'd be lying. It was easy to do—not encrypted, which makes a change."

Sam glanced at Bob. "You know what this means?"

He shrugged.

"Someone wanted us to find it."

"Claire or us?"

"You tell me. Maybe they tempted Claire there to pick up the USB stick and then thought better of it, deciding it was best to kill her."

"Again, that doesn't make sense. Why leave the evidence behind?"

"I don't know. It's up to us to find out. What information is on the file?"

"I'm going to have to leave that to you to sort through. I've got your email address; I'll send it to you now. Sorry, I've got work coming out of my ears. Although Des gave me the go-ahead to help you on this, I know what will happen if I don't have the other work ready for him that he's already requested for the day."

"Don't worry. It's early for us; we can go over it back at the station before the rest of the team arrive. We truly appreciate your assistance today, and thank you for squeezing us in."

"Thanks. There you go, all sent and out there in the ethernet, winging its way to you."

"Great. Thanks again. We'll get out of your hair now. Can I leave you to deal with the stick?"

"Consider it done." Mick ejected it from the machine and returned it to the plastic evidence bag.

. . .

BACK AT THE STATION, Sam raced ahead of Bob. He'd got caught up in traffic a few streets away. She switched on the lights and went through to her office to boot up her computer. She found the file sitting in her inbox.

"I hope you haven't opened it yet," Bob said from the doorway. "I thought we were going to go through it together?"

"We are, and no, I haven't opened it. I was checking it had arrived. Sort out the coffee, and I'll take a quick look at the post."

"Deal. Don't be tempted to open that file," he warned over his shoulder.

"Trust me. I'm your senior officer. Sometimes I think you forget that."

He laughed. "I don't. Because you won't let me."

Sam chuckled. That was true. She opened the five letters she'd received, sorted them into order of urgency and promptly returned them to her in-tray. "Perfect timing, thanks."

Bob placed a mug in front of her. "Do you want me to move my chair?"

"No, it'll be easier if I rotate the screen so both of us can see it." She took a sip from her mug and let out a satisfied moan. "That tastes divine. I barely touched the one Rhys made me this morning."

Bob raised an eyebrow. "Bit over the top; it's a cheap make and tastes nasty at the best of times. But each to their own."

Sam swivelled the screen. "Can you see it properly?"

"Yep, sort of."

They both sat on the edge of their seats as Sam opened the file marked *Pendle*. It was like entering an intriguing maze. Inside was a series of documents, patient reports and incident logs, all linked to Pendle House, a long-forgotten children's home that, during its time, had a dark reputation. Sam cast her mind back. She could vaguely remember the place. It had been closed for more than a decade, after a scandal had emerged involving missing files that hinted at abuse claims.

"Shit. I remember the scandal surrounding this place. Do you?"

"I think so. We need to find out what Claire was working on before she left yesterday."

They exited the room, taking their coffees with them, the file still open on Sam's computer. It was going to take the team a few days to go through what they'd discovered.

"Shit," Bob cussed. "I don't know her password to get into the system."

"Nor should you. Let me see if I can figure it out." Sam entered the obvious information, such as family members' names and dates of birth, which she located on Claire's personnel file. She eventually found the right combination and polished her fingers on the lapel of her jacket. "I did it. I broke the code."

"Smart arse," Bob muttered, rolling his eyes at her accomplishment.

"That's why I'm your senior officer, because I thought outside the box."

He raised his hand and coughed, discharging a single word: "Bullshit."

Sam pounded the keyboard and searched Claire's history tabs, the ones she'd recently closed. "Here we are. She's been searching the archives for articles relating to Pendle House. This tab was closed at twenty-one thirty yesterday."

"That has to be it."

Instinctively, Sam checked Claire's emails but saw nothing out of the ordinary in there.

"Check the Deleted box," Bob said.

Sam gasped when she saw that an email had arrived at twenty-one twenty the evening before. "Bingo!" She opened it and read the message from the unknown sender.

The heading read: **Four Must Fall,** and the message itself said:

YOU THINK **you're the only one who cares? This time, they will pay. One by one, with their lives. Starting with the doctor.**

.   .   .

Sam and Bob stared at each other, neither of them finding the appropriate words to say.

Bob pointed at Claire's phone on charge. "What an idiot. She didn't take it with her. She had no means of contacting either of us."

Sam shook her head and let out a long sigh. "Shit. You're right, she was out there on her own. She should have taken her phone with her." There was a tap on the window, startling Sam. "What was that?" A crow cawed sharply in the wind. It had grabbed their attention then flown off.

"Jesus, that's never happened before," Bob said. "Bloody spooky, if you ask me."

Shaken, Sam reached for Claire's phone and took a punt that the passcode would be Scott's birthday. She was right. She hit the messaging app and opened the last message Claire had received—the one that had ultimately led to the sergeant's death.

You're smart, *Claire. Smarter than most. That's why I picked you.*

But during your research, you overlooked something important. Do you want answers?

Meet me at Whitehaven Harbour. 10:15 p.m. Come alone.

"What the fuck!" Bob said, fury edging his voice. "Why didn't she contact us? What a stupid bitch. Sorry, but this should never have happened. She should have known better than to go alone. There's more to this than Claire just receiving a message."

"I think you're right. Hopefully, we'll find out what that is when we start digging into the file. I can't believe she lost her life because of this. There's no doubt about it, Bob. We're dealing with a sadistic killer, possibly one of the worst we've encountered over the years."

"No shit, Sherlock. I had kind of figured that out for myself."

Silence filled the room as both of them drank their coffee.

Sam finished hers and declared, "You were right, it was crap after all. Funny how our taste buds are different first thing in the morning."

"Yours might be, mine ain't, just saying."

"Whatever. There's nothing we can do until the rest of the team arrive."

"You could forward that file to me, and I could go through it."

"Okay. In the meantime, I'll deal with my post. Give me a shout when the others arrive. I'm not looking forward to sharing the news with them."

"I have to say, apart from the initial shock, you're taking it better than I thought you would."

"Maybe I'm still in shock. I'm also annoyed that Claire felt the need to go behind my back."

"Maybe she wanted to feel more appreciated. To be honest, she's been sat behind her desk for years, rarely getting out there to deal with any real police work."

"You think? The thought never even crossed my mind. Her skills were needed here; she was a whiz on the computer. I considered her to be a valued member of our team. She'd never let me down in the past. Right now, I feel she turned her back on me, and that's what got her killed."

"You're wrong. My take on it is that she wanted to prove herself, and with the information to hand, she went for it."

"In that case, she was a damn fool. More to the point, why the fuck did the killer contact her in the first place, instead of me?"

Bob's mouth twisted as he thought. "You've got me there."

Sam left the conversation because, by now, her blood was searing through her veins. She closed the office door behind her and rested her head back against it.

Why, Claire? Why did you go behind my back, our backs, like this?

Sam continued to her desk and completed her morning chore.

Bob knocked on the door half an hour later. He stuck his head in and said quietly, "You asked me to tell you when the rest of the team got here."

"Thanks. I'm coming now."

He stepped into the room. "Are we all right?"

"We? As in, you and me?"

"Yes. Only you stormed off before, and I thought I'd upset you."

"No more than usual." She smiled. "Sorry if it came across like that, mate. No, I'm angry about being deceived by Claire. I have no idea what we're about to uncover or why the killer chose to contact her directly."

Bob fell silent.

Sam knew when he had something on his mind. "Come on, what are you keeping from me?"

"Nothing. Umm... I think you should tell the team before they get stuck into their tasks for the day." He left the room.

Sam frowned. He seemed as if he had the weight of the world on his shoulders. Why?

Am I such an ogre that my team can't open up to me? What am I doing wrong?

She stretched out the knots in her back and ran a comb through her hair. Then she left the office to break the unwanted news. It was then that it hit her. She hadn't told Scott yet.

What the fuck is wrong with me?

She decided another ten minutes wouldn't hurt and braved telling the rest of the team first.

She entered the outer office, and Bob clapped to gain everyone's attention.

"Gather around, folks. There's been a development in the investigation overnight."

Nick raised his hand. "Sorry to interrupt, ma'am, but shouldn't we wait for Claire to arrive?"

Sam shook her head and inhaled a deep breath. "Umm... we're going to have to solve this case, and future cases, without her."

The other members of the team looked at each other, their brows furrowed, all of them perplexed.

"Are you all right?" Bob asked.

Sam swallowed down the lump that had appeared in her throat. "I will be. I'm sorry, team, this is the hardest thing I've ever had to tell you. Last night... our friend and colleague, Claire, was murdered."

The team's reaction was everything Sam had expected. They all fell silent for a second or two and then started bombarding her with questions, getting more and more irate when Sam remained quiet.

It was Bob who stepped in to calm things down. "Listen up, guys. I know you're as shocked as we are to hear the news. The truth is, we don't know who did this. Since the boss and I got here this morning, we've been trying to piece together Claire's final steps." He filled the rest of the team in.

Just listening to him, Sam felt drained.

She turned her back on the others and headed towards her office. "I'm sorry. I have to let Scott know the news now. I should have rung him earlier."

"Shouldn't you tell him face to face?" Bob called after her.

"You're right. I'll give him a call and see if he's at home. I know Claire told me he works away a lot of the time, overseeing developments out of the area."

"Yeah, you're right, he does," Bob agreed.

"I'll make the call in my office." She closed the door and stared out of the window for a few minutes, trying to summon up the right words. With her courage mustered, she sat behind her desk and slowly dialled Scott's mobile number.

"Yeah, Scott Owen."

There was a lot of background noise. Sam had to shout to be heard. "Scott, can you hear me?"

"Barely. Speak up. Who is this? Is that you, Claire?"

"No. How about now?"

"Nope. You're going to have to shout."

"I am shouting. This is DI Sam Cobbs, Claire's boss. Can you go somewhere less noisy? I need to speak with you. It's urgent," she added as an afterthought.

"Who is this? I can't hear you. Look, if you can't be bothered to shout then I'm hanging up."

"Scott. Can you hear me now?" Sam shouted even louder, straining her vocal cords.

The door burst open seconds later, and Bob stood in the doorway, looking concerned. Sam gave him the thumbs-up. He backed out of the room again.

"Yes, I can hear you. Who is this?"

"It's Sam Cobbs, Claire's boss."

"Her boss? What do you want? Is she at work?"

"Are you away at the moment?"

"I should be home in a few hours. Why?"

Sam inhaled and exhaled a few deep breaths. "It's important I speak with you."

"About what?"

There was a loud bang in the distance.

Scott shouted. "For fuck's sake. Be more careful; that's coming out of your wages, Les."

Sam held the phone away from her ear. *This is a ridiculous way to hold a conversation of this magnitude. Nope, I refuse to do it.*

"Scott, I can tell you're really busy there," Sam yelled. "Can you give me a call when you return home?"

"Yeah. Okay. I'll do that. Is Claire all right?"

"I'll talk to you later." Sam ended the call before he could say anything else. She leaned her head back and released a frustrated sigh. "Jesus, that was hard work." She removed the bottle of water from her drawer and eased her sore throat before she joined the rest of the team.

"How did he take it?" Bob asked.

"It wasn't the right time to tell him. He was on site. I wasn't prepared to shout the information down the phone at him."

"Ah, gotcha. Yeah, I think you did the right thing. When are you going to tell him?"

"He's back in a couple of hours. I've asked him to give me a call when he gets home. I'm going to be on tenterhooks until then."

"I don't think you're going to get a chance to. I need to speak to you privately."

"Can it wait? I need to bring the DCI up to date."

Bob shook his head and walked past her and into her office. Sam glanced around the rest of the team. They all avoided eye contact with her, making her dread what Bob was about to tell her. She marched into her office and closed the door. She sat opposite her partner and searched his eyes for the answer to her unspoken question.

"I've forgotten something. Bear with me." He jumped out of his seat and darted out of the room. He came back holding a sheet of paper.

"This looks ominous. Does this have something to do directly with Claire?"

"Not this, not exactly. Umm... I'm not sure how to tell you this."

Sam's patience was already tighter than a prison cell door at lights out. "Get on with it, Bob. I can't stand the suspense much longer, and don't forget I'm eager to see the DCI."

"Sorry, I'll get to the point. Rhys's name crops up in the file."

Sam frowned and shook her head. "What?" She opened the file on the computer and scrolled through it to check for herself. "Holy shit balls! What the fuck?"

"Have you found it?"

"Shh... I'm reading it now," she said, preferring to read from the screen for herself rather than what he'd printed out, as if it made any difference. It didn't—the fact was there in black and white. Rhys did a placement at Pendle during his time at university. Sara stared at her partner and muttered, "He's never mentioned it."

"Why would he?"

"True. Oh shit! What else are we going to bloody uncover, Bob?"

He fidgeted awkwardly in his seat, and she could tell he was keeping quiet about something else.

"Let me have it."

"I couldn't resist it. I know you only conducted a brief search of Claire's computer earlier. Well, I took the liberty of digging a bit deeper and..."

"And? Damn, I swear you can be frustrating as hell at times. Just give me the facts without all the drama attached."

His mouth gaped open for a second or two.

"Sorry, me having a go at you isn't going to help matters, is it?"

"Apology accepted. Please, you have to remember I'm on your side, Sam."

"I don't need reminding."

He cocked an eyebrow. "Don't you?"

"Bob," she warned, the heat warming up her veins once more.

"Okay, are you ready for this?"

She resisted the urge to roll her eyes again.

"All right, here we go. I checked the recent files Claire had created and found one that she had encrypted."

"What? Why would she do that? Dumb question one thousand and one coming up. Do we know what was on it?"

Bob raised a finger. "As it happens, we do. It's marked, REDACTED STAFF LIST."

She shook her head and went over the information they had discovered so far. "What the fuck. We need to see if Mick at the lab will do us a second favour today. Can you sort that for me while I bring Armstrong up to date?"

"Go for it. I can send him the file rather than go over there. At least, I should be able to do it."

Bob shot out of the room to deal with the task. Sam left her chair and followed him into the outer office and up the corridor, taking a chance that DCI Alan Armstrong was available to see her. Heidi, his efficient secretary, smiled as she entered the office.

"Sorry to disturb you, Heidi. I don't suppose the boss can squeeze me in for a brief chat, can he?"

Heidi winked. "He's just finished a call and doesn't have another one lined up for about an hour. Let me ask the question." She rose from her seat and knocked on the DCI's door. "Sorry to trouble you, sir. DI Cobbs is here. She'd like a word with you, if you have time to see her."

"I have. I'd welcome the break after dealing with the superintendent on the last call. Send her in. I'm sure the inspector would *love* one of our special coffees, if you wouldn't mind arranging that for us, Heidi?"

"My pleasure, sir." Heidi walked away from the door and gestured for Sam to enter the room.

"A coffee would be a great idea. Thanks, Heidi."

"I'll get that sorted right away. Good luck."

"Hello, Sam. This is a nice surprise. What's up?"

Sam waited until she was sitting opposite him before she revealed the truth behind her visit. "This is hard for me to say, sir..."

"No, I won't accept it."

Confused, Sam said, "Accept what, sir?"

"Your resignation. If that's what your visit is all about."

"It isn't, and I would never give up on the job I love more than life itself, sir. No matter how tempting it might be during a tough investigation."

"Ah, okay. I was assuming that would be the case. Your expression is very grave today. Should I prepare myself for bad news?"

"It's with a heavy heart that I have to tell you that a member of my team was killed last night."

Her words hit him like a fist to the jaw, knocking him backwards into the chair. After a moment or two, he recovered and bounced upright again. "Tell me how it happened."

She revealed what she knew about the incident and what she and Bob had discovered since they'd arrived at work that morning.

"Bloody hell. Are you all right, Sam?"

"I think so. I've slotted into professional mode. I'm conscious about keeping at it, fearing that if I stop, it might hit me harder."

"Shit! I can understand that. I've never had a reason to tell you this before, but years ago, when I started off on the beat—I know, that was long before your time—my partner was stabbed by a youth. I was there, luckily, right beside him. I knew what to do in the emergency and managed to keep him alive until they got him to hospital. The youth had punctured my partner's lung, and Ron faded fast once he was taken to A and E. I've always felt guilty about the incident. I asked myself over and over: why did it happen to him and not to me? Ron was six months away from his retirement. All those years on the Force, and he never got to enjoy the benefits of his copper's pension."

"That's so sad. I'm sorry to hear that, sir. It's true what they say: we continue to put our lives on the line daily in order to protect the public, not that it's appreciated by some members of the public."

"It's what we signed up for, but in reality, it knocks us sideways when we have to deal with the consequences of things going wrong. Are you and your team up for working the case?"

"I'm aware that we should hand it over, sir, but I'd feel bad letting someone else deal with it. Claire was a great officer and a close colleague. I know I'm speaking on behalf of the rest of my team when I say this, but we'd feel we were letting her down if we didn't find the killer."

"I'll run it past the super and let you know what he has to say. Don't worry, I'll make sure he appreciates the importance behind your decision to keep working the investigation."

"Thank you. That means a lot, sir."

"Sorry if this sounds flippant. How did her family take it? Was she married?"

"Her husband is away. He's due back in a few hours. I tried to tell him over the phone, but the site was too noisy. In the end, I decided to back off and visit him later, once he's home. He'll probably hit the roof when he finds out that I've delayed telling him, but I'm prepared for the backlash. Our whole conversation was conducted by us shouting. It just seemed inappropriate to continue the conversation."

"I wholeheartedly agree with you."

The door opened, and Heidi brought the coffees in.

"Thank you, Heidi," Armstrong said. He slid the cup and saucer in front of Sam.

Sam's mind had wandered while Heidi had delivered the drinks. *The email, the message from the killer. The precision of the kills. The victims the killer had chosen. Someone is hunting people connected to Pendle House, and now... the discovery of Rhys's name on that list. What if he's next? What if...?*

"Sam, are you still with me?"

"Sorry, sir. I was going over all the information that has come to light since we found DS Owen's body this morning."

"What aren't you telling me?"

Her head bowed. Should she tell him? Did he have a right to know that her fella might be involved in a scandal they knew very little about yet?

"I suppose I'm just working through the details in my mind, trying to sort out where we should turn next."

"All that can wait for now. Your priority remains to tell the next of kin."

"I'm aware of that, sir, and I'd be round there like a shot to tell Scott if he were available."

"I know you would. It wasn't a criticism. Drink your coffee. I'm going to call the superintendent while you're here."

"I can leave the room if you'd rather, sir."

"Nonsense. Stay there and enjoy your drink."

Sam sipped the rich coffee and, without realising she was doing it, let out a satisfied moan. Her coffee went down well, compared to the one Bob had made her earlier. She couldn't believe it was after eleven and she was only just having her third cup of the day. She drifted off again, her thoughts lying with the investigation, blocking out the conversation the DCI was having until he hung up.

"That's settled. He took some persuading, but he finally agreed, on one proviso."

Here it comes. "Oh, and what's that?"

"That I'm involved every step of the way."

Sam pinned a smile in place and lied through her teeth, hoping he wouldn't see through her. "Oh, that'd be great to be working alongside you, sir."

"Don't lie, Inspector. We both know how livid you are at the prospect. I'm going to leave you to deal with the investigation, but you must, and I can't emphasise this enough, you must tell me if anything untoward is on the horizon. I don't want to be told something major has happened after the event has occurred. Am I making myself clear here?"

"Of course. Thank you for trusting me and my team. We won't let you down."

"I have every confidence in you. Now, we're going to need to sort out how to fill Claire's shoes. You've already got a new member of the team, haven't you?"

"Yes, Nick, the former desk sergeant. He seems to have slotted in nicely already. It's only been a few weeks. I'm not sure who will be able to replace Claire. She was our whiz on the computer and mainly remained at her desk all day. I considered her role a key one on the team."

"So, what you're telling me is that an admin-led position would be best for you and the team?"

"Given the choice, yes."

"Leave it with me. I'll have a word with HR and get back to you."

"Thanks, sir." Sam downed the rest of her coffee and bid her boss farewell. "Sorry to be the bearer of bad news this morning."

"Shit happens as we both know in this game. Don't forget what I said. Any major issues, you must run them past me. I'm putting all my trust in you, Sam."

"I know you are. I won't let you down, sir. I promise."

"Glad to hear it. I'll expect an update at the end of each working day until this investigation is over."

Sam groaned inside. *As if my job isn't difficult enough as it is.* "Consider it done. Thanks for having my back, sir. I'll pass on your condolences to the rest of the team."

"Please do."

Sam left the office and thanked Heidi for supplying her with the best cup of coffee she was likely to receive that day. On her journey back up the corridor, all she could think about was Rhys's suspected involvement with Pendle House and what impact that knowledge was going to have on their relationship.

· · ·

THE CALL CAME in from Scott two hours later. He was in the car on his way home. Sam arranged to meet him at his house. She took Bob with her for moral support.

Scott answered the door and looked daggers at both of them. "I demand to know what's going on. I've tried ringing Claire several times, and she's ignoring my calls. She never does that. We're very close."

And yet you weren't concerned enough to call the station yesterday when she didn't come home from work. Stop it! He was working away from home; give the guy a chance.

"Sorry, is it possible for us to come in, Scott?"

"If you must. You're here to tell me bad news, aren't you? Is she alive?"

He stepped back and allowed Sam and Bob to enter. They followed him into a spacious modern lounge.

He flopped into the armchair and gestured for them to sit on the sofa. "You haven't answered me."

"I'm sorry, Scott. You're right, the news isn't good. Bob and I were called out to an incident that had happened at the harbour in Whitehaven..."

"Get on with it," he snarled.

"Take it easy, mate," Bob interjected. "Sam's doing her best here."

"Let's get one thing straight: I'm not your mate. I don't really know you. You're Claire's colleagues, not mine. So, let's not beat about the bush here. Tell me the truth."

Sam sighed. "I'm sorry, but the incident involved Claire. She was found floating in the harbour."

Scott stared at her, disbelief etched into his face. "What are you saying? That she's dead?"

Sam gulped and swallowed down the bile that was burning her throat. "I'm so sorry. We're all devastated by the news of her death. She was a valued member of our team."

"I don't need your sympathy. Is it worth me asking what happened? Why she was at the harbour? Did she go alone? Was she chasing someone?"

"The clues are sketchy at the moment. I can't really go into detail right now. She was working off her own bat, though, not on my instructions."

"What are you talking about? Are you calling her bent?"

"No, not at all. Like I said, there's more to this than we can explain. It's a difficult one. I'm sorry, but the fact is that Claire wasn't told to go there last night. I would never have sent a member of my team off somewhere alone, not at that time of night."

"Get out. You're telling me you know nothing. Why are you here?"

"I'm trying to explain it as I see it."

"Come back when you know what you're talking about. I'm going to put in a complaint."

"There's no need for that, Scott," Bob said. "Sam and the rest of the team, we're all doing our best to find out why Claire took it upon herself to chase up a lead we've yet to discover."

He glared at Bob and rose from his seat. "I've told you to leave."

With that, he threw them out of the house. It had been an upsetting experience for Sam, and Bob didn't appear to be faring much better either.

Bob rubbed her arm as they walked towards their respective cars. "He'll calm down, eventually."

"He's got every right to be upset with me. Blimey, I'm upset with myself, and I'm as angry as fuck about Claire going behind my back."

"We don't know what her motive was, Sam."

"I know. I'll see you in the morning. Have a good evening."

"I doubt it. Take care, Sam. None of this is your fault."

"Thanks, Bob. See you tomorrow."

SAM WENT HOME that evening and immediately took Tilly out to the park for a long walk, more to clear her head than anything else. Tilly was eager to run after the squirrels, but Sam felt it was far too soon to let the little one off the lead yet, especially as her recall wasn't really showing signs of improvement. She sat on the bench, Tilly at her feet, and reflected on how her day had panned out. From the early morning discovery of Claire's body in the harbour, to finding out that she had been digging into information about Pendle House behind Sam's back. That news might sound insignificant to some of her colleagues ranking higher than inspector, but to her, it had proved to be a kick in the teeth.

Now she had the daunting task of having the dreaded conversation with Rhys about his involvement at the notorious children's home.

Tilly gently pawed at Sam's leg and whined. Sam bent to kiss the tip of her cute nose and hugged her. "Sorry, sweetie, am I ignoring you? Let's go home."

She left the bench and spotted Rhys entering the park with Casper. "Hi, I thought I might find you here. I nipped home to prepare dinner. It's already to go when we get home."

"Thanks. That'll save me a job when I get in. I'll see you back there." With that, she walked off.

She could imagine the shock on his face at her departure. To be fair, she couldn't give a toss and was determined not to look back, despite him calling out her name. Tears bulged and trickled onto her cheeks. Right now, she felt as miserable as sin.

"Come on, Tilly. Let's go home. I'll give you one of your special treats to make up for letting you down on your walk."

Tilly trotted along beside her without a care in the world, the way it should be for a dog. It got Sam wondering what horrors her little rescue dog had dealt with back in Romania before she was swooped off the streets and put into the care of the sanctuary. Dogs deserved a better life than most were given.

Sonny had had the best life ever, or had he? He should have spent his days with me, not Doreen, but work commitments prevented that from happening. Now Tilly's in the same boat. Stop it! No regrets, remember? I've saved Tilly from a life of hell. She loves and appreciates all that I've done for her ever since. She adores Doreen as well, so it's a win-win situation.

Sam approached the row of cottages and summoned up a lack-lustre smile as she waved at Doreen, who was watching out for them to return. They gave each other a thumbs-up and blew kisses.

"See you in the morning," Sam mouthed.

Inside the cottage, Sam removed Tilly's new harness before taking off her own shoes and jacket. Then Tilly followed her into the kitchen to the treat cupboard. Sam withdrew the packet of sausage-shaped morsels. She cut off a link and gave it to Tilly to eat in the garden. Sam had a mooch around the kitchen to see what preparation Rhys had made for dinner. Chicken stir-fry. At any other time, she would have been thrilled with the menu. Not so much today, though. Her appetite had been absent all day. She cast her mind back to what she had consumed at work. It amounted to half a sandwich that Bob had picked up from the baker's. He'd eaten the rest after she pushed it aside. Leaving the kitchen door open for Tilly to come and find her once she'd finished the treat, she went upstairs to get changed.

She was surprised to hear the front door open and slam ten minutes later and prepared herself for a tongue-lashing from Rhys. His footsteps sounded on the stairs. Sam slipped her velour top over her head and was brushing her hair when he appeared in the doorway.

"Do you mind telling me what I've done wrong?"

"Nothing. Why?"

"Why? You really need to ask that question after the way you've just blanked me at the park, as if I were a complete stranger, I might add?"

"I didn't."

He crossed the room and spun her around to face him. "Don't lie. What the hell is going on?"

Sam wriggled out of his grip and tripped over Casper in her attempt to get away from him. She landed on her backside on the floor. "Leave me alone. I need time to think."

Rhys shooed Casper out of the way and held out a hand to help her to her feet. Sam grudgingly accepted it and brushed herself down.

"Why am I in the doghouse? I barely saw you this morning and, as far as I can remember, everything was all right between us when we went to bed last night. Forgive me if I'm confused, but I need to know what's happened to make you turn against me since then."

"We'll discuss it after dinner. I haven't eaten much today, and I'm feeling light-headed."

"Is that why you fell? Are you sure you don't need to see a doctor? Is there something medically wrong with you, and you're too scared to tell me in case I dump you? Is that it, Sam?"

"No. Nothing could be further from the truth. I'm fit and healthy. A lot has happened today, and I need to get my head around it before I tell you what's going on."

"And yet, you can treat me like shit while we're out. How in the world do I deserve that? After all we've been through together, I never, ever, thought you would turn your back on me, literally, and refuse to speak to me."

"I'm sorry." She ran out of the bedroom and down the stairs.

He followed her and found her watching Tilly, who was attacking a shrub in the garden, clearly uninterested in the treat she'd just been given.

"No, Tilly," he shouted from behind her, scaring Sam half to death. "You shouldn't let her get away with that."

"I'm sorry," she apologised for the second time in as many minutes.

"Are you going to tell me what's wrong?"

Tilly ran past them and sat down by her bowl.

"I'll feed the dogs and then tell you."

"Okay. Am I cooking for two tonight, or are you going to give my food a miss, too?" he asked. Hurt swam in his eyes even though he still managed a hint of a smile.

Sam avoided looking at him, her heart hurting the most it had in years. She'd had a lot to deal with of late, still feeling the loss of Sonny, and now coping with Claire's death. The meeting with Scott had left her feeling distraught. She'd needed her time at the park with Tilly, hoping it would help her put life back into perspective, and it probably would have, if only Rhys hadn't turned up. It was the secrets and lies she was struggling with. However, Rhys hadn't got a clue about what had taken place during the day, and she didn't have it in her to tell him what Bob had discovered. Not yet, not without them digging deeper into that file. Breaking the news to Scott had almost broken her. She hadn't expected him to react so vehemently. Although his anger was understandable, Sam couldn't wait to get away from him.

"How much do you want?" Rhys said.

"The usual, maybe a little less than normal." Sam fed the dogs and filled up their water bowls, then set the table.

Rhys put the plate in front of her.

"Thank you," she whispered, then tucked into her meal, which smelt delicious.

"Are you going to tell me what's wrong now? Is this about Claire's death?"

She stared at her plate. "Yes, but that's not all. Sorry, I'm not ready to discuss what else has come to light; it's too raw right now."

"I'm not sure what that means. We don't have to talk about it. In your own time. I'm not going to push you, sweetheart. Just know that I'm here for you."

"Thank you."

She didn't look up from her plate, and they continued to eat in silence. She had a hell of a lot of soul searching to do before she could summon up the courage to ask him about his involvement with Pendle House. It was obvious there was more to that establishment than they had discovered so far, and she felt that if she asked him outright what he knew about it, she wasn't in the right frame of mind to tell whether he was being truthful or not. To say she was confused would be wrong. However, she was on the fence, with a pointy bit sticking up her backside, causing her major discomfort.

"What would you like to do this evening?" Rhys asked as he pushed his empty plate aside.

"I need to make some notes. Your day might be over, but when a copper is murdered, my part in the investigation multiplies tenfold."

"I can imagine. I'm sorry you're having to deal with this shit, Sam. A gentle reminder that I'm here if you need to run anything past me."

"I won't. I got to be an inspector years ago, without you or anyone else to assist me," Sam snapped back, leaving the table. She ran upstairs and closed the bedroom door behind her, leaving him to clear up the kitchen and to occupy the dogs for the rest of the evening. A tinge of guilt crept in, but she quickly suppressed it.

Why should I feel guilty? If he's involved in what went on at that school... well, I'm appalled and feel grossly let down by him.

And if he's not? Her second inner voice asked the other important question that had been prodding her all day.

5

Sam received the call that another body had been found at a building site on the edge of Workington. She had no hesitation in jumping in the car with Bob in tow and travelling to the scene.

"I can see how worked up you're getting about this by the colour of your knuckles. Just a reminder, we don't yet know if this murder is connected to the investigation."

"I'm well aware of that fact. But here's the thing: I stopped believing in coincidences not long after I graduated from training school."

"All right, that was uncalled for. There's no need to be sarcastic just because I state the obvious now and again."

"I wouldn't mind if that were the case. 'Now and again' means something entirely different in your book than it does in mine."

Bob crossed his arms and glanced out of the side window until they were much closer to the location. "I'm sorry for stating the obvious."

"Apology accepted. This part is going to hurt... and I'm sorry for having a go at you."

"Is this about what happened last night, when you got home?"

She frowned and shot him a quick look before she returned her gaze to the road ahead. "Meaning?"

"What the fuck? You didn't tackle Rhys about what we found, did you?"

Her grip tightened around the steering wheel.

"No need to answer. Actions speak louder than words."

Sam sighed. "I couldn't. God help me, I wanted to, but my anger got the better of me. After we'd eaten, I ended up shutting myself away in the bedroom for the rest of the evening."

"I don't get it. Why?"

"Because I was too scared to start the conversation with him. We don't have enough evidence against him, and I wasn't sure how I wanted to proceed. Just finding his name in a file isn't enough to be suspicious of him, and yet last night, I treated him like a convicted criminal."

"Jesus, Sam. Why?"

"Stop bloody asking me that. Because..."

"What? Just because, or am I missing what you're trying to say here?"

"Because for the first time in my life, I'm confused. No, make that dumbfounded beyond words that Claire chose not to confide in me, went behind my back and ended up..."

"Dead! You can say the word. It doesn't stop you normally. It's generally part of our usual vocabulary, especially during an investigation."

"All right, Bob, there's no need for the added sarcasm. I'm feeling shit enough about this case as it is."

"I'm sorry. At the end of the day, we've got a job to do. Would you rather it was me who tackled Rhys?"

"No. I'll do it in my own time. First, we need to find out how deep this goes and what Claire's involvement was in it." She drew onto the road leading to the building site. "Let's leave this conversation here, for now."

"We will definitely revisit it, though. We have to, Sam. All you're doing by avoiding the obvious is tying yourself into knots."

"I hear you." She parked behind two patrol cars.

Four officers were trying to control a crowd of workmen, and things appeared to be getting heated.

"We'd better shake a leg or two and get in there to help out."

"I'm sensing things might escalate soon. My advice would be for you to stay back."

"Thanks for your concern. I happen to believe the opposite would be better to ease the tension here."

They exited the car, and Bob shrugged at her.

"You're the boss."

"Exactly." She grinned and marched towards the group. "Who's in charge here?"

An older man raised his hand. "I'm the foreman."

"Can I have a chat with you in private?" Sam pointed at a free spot not ten feet away.

He followed her, and the crowd quietened down behind them.

"Sorry, I didn't catch your name?"

"Likewise, and that's because I didn't give it. I'm Nigel Bowman."

"Forgive me, Mr Bowman. I'm Detective Inspector Sam Cobbs. Can you tell me what all this commotion is about?"

"The men are keen to get back to work. We're on a tight schedule, and they're worried their bonuses will be affected."

"Ah, I see. Whilst I can understand where they are coming from, until the pathologist and his team have carried out the necessary work at the crime scene, the site is going to be off limits to everyone."

He growled and shook his head. "I hope you're ready for the uproar that's going to cause when I break the news to them."

"Surely, that'll be down to you to control your men, won't it?"

"I'll do my best. The thing is, I've only just been promoted and..."

"You haven't earnt their respect yet. Is that what you're hinting at?"

"Yes, that's it in a nutshell."

"And what if your boss was down here, telling you to pack up and leave? Would they still be standing their ground?"

"No, they wouldn't. Sorry, I'll send them home. Any idea how long your team are going to be on site?"

"For as long as it takes. I suggest a minimum of two days."

Bowman ran a hand through what little hair he had left. "Jesus, that's taking the piss."

"Let me put it this way: if it were a member of your family who had been murdered, you'd expect the experts to carry out their jobs efficiently and quickly, wouldn't you?"

He raised a hand and turned to walk away. "Enough said. I'll give them their marching orders."

"Thank you. We really appreciate your cooperation."

"I'll do my best and hope that anarchy doesn't break out. I must have been an idiot to have accepted this job at the end of last week," he muttered as he walked away.

"Everything all right?" Bob asked as he joined her.

"We'll soon find out. Poor bloke has his back against the wall. Be prepared to intervene. He's new to the job and is about to tell them to go home and risk losing their bonuses."

Bob shrugged. "Not everything in life is that cut and dried, is it? Sometimes people throw a spanner in the works."

"So true."

They watched as the foreman called for the group's attention and issued the bad news. The crowd of men surged towards him, but Bowman stood firm and ended up shouting at them. A few of his colleagues instantly backed down; the others needed to think it through first.

"Crisis averted," Bob whispered.

"We'll see how long that lasts."

"Ah, here's Des and the team now. Let's help to disperse this crowd quickly."

Bob jumped into action and assisted the foreman with his authoritarian voice in full swing. "Come on, gents. Do as you're told now. The professionals are waiting to get to the crime scene. The sooner you allow them access, the quicker you'll be able to get back to work, right?"

The men released a mixture of groans and murmurings of discontent, until they reluctantly gave up the fight and drifted off.

Relieved, Sam and Bob slipped on their protective suits but left their shoe coverings off until they were closer to the scene. Bob handed Sam a pair of gloves, and they made their way over to Des's van.

"Good morning. Don't ask; we haven't had a chance to view the body yet. We've been too busy negotiating with the workforce. Don't shoot the messenger, but they're working on a tight schedule and have been promised a bonus if they finish early."

"Not my problem. We'll take as long as necessary to assess the crime scene. You know that as well as I do, Inspector."

"I know. I told them as much. All right if we head over there and have a look for ourselves?"

"As long as you don't approach the victim. I'm assuming he's been confirmed dead if we've been called in?"

"He must be. We haven't been here long ourselves," she replied.

Sam nudged Bob, and they set off.

"I sometimes wonder if I'm talking a foreign language," she said. "I seem to be repeating myself a lot lately."

"You are? I hadn't noticed. No more than usual anyway." His jibe earned him a dig in the ribs.

"Don't push me, matey."

"It was a joke, Mrs Sensitive."

They approached the side of the building where the foreman had told Bob the body was situated. The second Sam rounded the corner, she froze. There, tied to the scaffolding planks, was a man in a navy-blue suit. The air was silent and raw with tension. Sam could see there was a placard on his chest but struggled to read it.

"Can you see what it says?"

"*Buried the truth.*"

Sam exhaled a large breath and continued to walk towards the body. It wasn't until she got to within ten feet of the victim that she noticed his head was lying at an odd angle and his lips had been stitched together. She stepped closer until the victim came fully into focus. The placard wasn't pinned to his chest; it had been attached with a thick nail. "Fuck, is that what I think it is?"

"Yep. Let's hope it was nailed in place *after* he took his last breath."

"Me too."

Rustling behind her announced Des's arrival. "Right, what have we got he...? Ouch, that's not good. Hurry up, men. Let's get this area sectioned off. I need a partial tent erected at least. This victim has had an audience for too long as it is. Poor bloke."

"We haven't been near him. Can you give him a quick search for ID?

"On it now." Des slipped his hand into the man's jacket pockets and drew a blank. "Nothing in either of those." He stepped around the side and patted down the back of the victim. "Ah, here we are."

Sam took a few steps closer while Bob withdrew his notebook, ready to jot down the information.

"Stephen Weller. As well as his driving licence, there's a council ID. He's a planning officer."

"Shit. Does that mean he was here in an official capacity, or did the killer bring him here to make a statement?" Sam asked, her voice trailing off as her thoughts began to run riot, not for the first time during this investigation.

"We have no way of knowing. What is clear is that the other murders are connected to this one."

"That much is obvious," Bob said without engaging his brain first.

Des ignored him and proceeded to read out the address on the driving licence. "Fifty-six Sillcroft Road, Barepot."

"Thanks. We'll take a drive over there once we've finished here. Can you tell us how long he's been dead?"

"Without carrying out the usual tests on the organs, it's going to be hard to say. You'll need to find out what time the site was closed down last night. I'm assuming they worked here yesterday. Do we know what time the body was found?"

Sam glanced at Bob. "I'm on my way," he shouted, sprinting back to the group of builders. He returned after speaking with the foreman and said, "Site closed at five last night. They showed up again at seven-thirty but didn't discover the body until gone eight."

"Did they see anyone hanging around?" Sam asked.

"Nope, I checked."

"So, sometime between what? Sixish and seven-thirty would be my logical answer," Des grinned.

Sam pulled a face, avoiding the temptation to poke her tongue out at him. She scanned the area. It seemed secure enough, and the knowledge that the front of the site would have been locked at the end of the builders' shift was a cause of concern for her.

"How did he get here?"

"And more to the point, how did the killer?" Des added. "Hang on, is that something written on the fence over there?"

He pointed in the distance, but Sam's eyesight was letting her down again. She walked towards it and was still quite a distance from the fence when Bob announced, "It's the number three."

"The third victim," Sam muttered.

"Here's the thing," Bob started. He peered over his shoulder, making sure they were alone, then continued. "I recognise the name."

"You do? How? Because of his job?"

"I remember reading it in the file. He was on the local authority board back when Pendle House was shut down. I stand corrected, but I think it was his signature on the redevelopment plans for the site."

"What was erected in its place? Can you recall?"

Bob's nod increased in tempo. "Luxury flats."

"Say no more. I suggest backhanders were at play then. Hmm... convenient there's no longer a site left for us to investigate."

"Yep, very convenient."

"The killer isn't just targeting those involved. I believe they're making a statement."

"This sign, along with the others we've found, is written in blood."

"They're rewriting the past in blood," Sam whispered. "Okay, you know what's next?"

"We need to shoot over and break the news to the next of kin," Bob said.

. . .

THEY LEFT the scene after ensuring that the officers on site had taken down all the personal information from the builders, so that statements could be collected from them within the next few days.

"Another day, and another murder to add to the list. Bob, can you ring the station and put Nick on the case? Ask him to do the background checks on Weller. Let's see what he's been up to over the years, in case anything else rears its head."

"On it now." Bob issued the instructions to Nick and then ended the call. "All in hand. Nick wanted me to pass on his gratitude for trusting him with such an important task. He also wanted me to tell you that he won't let you down."

"I know he won't. Hmm... maybe he'd be up for taking on Claire's role in the team."

"Good idea. I bet he wouldn't mind that. Unless he was looking forward to getting his chance to be out there on the streets, getting stuck in and making the arrests."

"I'll have a word with him when we get back. I suppose it depends on what his computer skills are like."

"Well, Oliver and Liam can help out occasionally on that front, too."

Sam parked the car outside Weller's home. They exited the vehicle.

"We can sort it when we get back, before Armstrong finds us a replacement. Let's hope someone is at home." Sam entered the small front garden.

There was an old man tending to his lawn next door. He stopped cutting the grass and glanced up. "I wouldn't bother. He's not in. His car isn't in the drive."

"Ah, okay. What about his wife?" Sam held up her badge. "DI Sam Cobbs."

"They split up a few months ago. She lives in Workington, not sure where. My wife will know, though." He opened the front door and bellowed, "Renee, can you come out here, please?"

A grey-haired woman appeared in the doorway. She wiped her hands on the flowered apron she was wearing. "What do you want?"

"These two are police officers. They want Wendy's address. Can you give it to them? I'm busy cutting the lawn."

"And I'm busy making your dinner, or doesn't that count?"

He tutted and started up the mower again.

His wife raised a finger and dipped back into the house. She returned with an address book a few seconds later. "Ah, yes, here we are."

Bob poised his pen over his notebook.

"Block C, flat twenty-four, Greenacre Terrace. Do you know it?"

"I do. Thanks for the information," Bob replied. "Do you know if she's likely to be at home?"

"Yes. I saw her the other day. She told me she hadn't had much luck finding a job, but she's not in a rush either, because Stephen was paying the rent and giving her a healthy allowance to live on for the next few months."

"Thanks, that's great information," Sam said.

THEY DROVE to the wife's address and found the flat they were looking for. It was up four flights of stairs, and the lift was out of order. Sam had to listen to Bob complain all the way up.

Finally, on the last flight of steps, she said, "Give it a rest, will you?"

"Sorry. I thought I was fit until I started climbing these frigging steps. I need to take out another gym membership."

"Hang on. I thought you'd recently bought a home gym."

His mouth twisted, and his nose wrinkled. "How do you do that?"

"Do what?" Sam paused and faced him on the landing.

"Retain trash information like that?"

She laughed. "You're unbelievable, the crap you come out with. Did you buy a gym or not?"

"I did. I just haven't got around to setting it up, yet. That's going to be a bloody workout in itself before I get to use the damn thing."

"Haven't you got a friend who can help you?"

"I might have. Number twenty-four should be on the right up ahead."

"Ah, the swift change of subject. That's one thing you're the master of, if not building a home gym. Blooming heck, how difficult can it be to screw a few bolts together?"

"Difficult enough. Back to business, eh? Before we have one of our notorious arguments."

"Bollocks. Since when do we argue?"

"All the time."

She sniggered and led the way. The door was opened by a woman in her forties wearing a towelling robe.

"Oh, sorry. Did we have an appointment?"

Sam produced her warrant card. "I'm Detective Inspector Sam Cobbs, and this is Detective Sergeant Bob Jones. Would it be all right if we came in and spoke with you, Mrs Weller?"

"I don't understand. What's this about?"

"Your husband. Or should I say, your estranged husband?"

"How does what Stephen gets up to now concern me? We're separated."

"It would be better if we spoke inside."

"If I must. I have to say, anything that man has done shouldn't reflect badly on me." She gestured for them to enter. "Close the door behind you."

Bob did as instructed, and they followed her up the narrow hallway. By the look of things, this flat was a comedown from the home she had shared with her husband.

"This is temporary until the house is sold. Then I get fifty percent of the pot, which will enable me to at least put a substantial deposit down on another house."

"Glad to hear it. Would you mind if we take a seat?"

"As long as you're not expecting a drink. I've run out of milk. I need to go to the supermarket later."

"Don't worry, we're fine." Sam waited for her to sit and then hit her with the news. "I'm sorry to have to inform you, but your husband's body was found first thing this morning."

"His body?" After a slight delay, she asked, "Are you telling me he's dead?"

Sam nodded. "Yes. I know you're separated. I was wondering if you could tell me whether his parents are alive, or if he has any siblings you think should be informed."

"No. He was an only child. He told me his parents died when he was in his twenties."

"Ah, I see. And are there no other distant relatives you can think of who we should inform?"

"No. He was a bit of a loner. Didn't get on with his family and saw them as leeches. I got the impression he thought the same of me, come the end."

"Is that why you split up?"

"Yes. There comes a point in one's life when you need to put your foot down and think of yourself. The trouble with Stephen was, I suppose you'd call him self-absorbed. He spent years living on his nerves, working all sorts of unsociable hours for that damn council. He didn't enjoy his job; he did it because he had to."

"Was he on any medication?"

"Yes, he was. Don't ask me what type. He kept it from me. The shutters came down years ago. We should have separated back then. It was foolish of me to stay in the belief that he might change."

"Do you think the fact that he was on medication has changed him over the years?"

"Hard to say. He was always a difficult man to read, even before we got married. Maybe I should have considered that before our wedding day. You know how it is; you tend to put all the doubts you have about your partner to one side..."

"Just to have a wedding day?"

"Yes. Now that I've said it out loud, I realise how shallow that sounds. Sorry."

"There's no need for you to apologise."

"I suppose I should ask how he died."

"I can't go into details, but what I can tell you is that we're treating his death as suspicious."

A hand slapped against her chest, and she let out a gasp. "Does that mean he was murdered? Who? Why?"

"It does. That's what we need to find out. I appreciate how difficult and possibly awkward this is for you, but is there anything, anything at all, you can tell us that you think might help?"

"What would I know about someone wanting to murder him? Yes, I admit I've often felt the need to do it over the years, but going through with it would have been a different kettle of fish. Oh my... do you think it was to do with his job?"

"What makes you say that?" Sam asked, her interest piqued.

"I got the impression that he did a lot of work out of hours."

"Such as?"

"You know, there were always a lot of meetings to attend in the evenings. I asked him time and time again what they were about and why they needed to be held out of hours."

"And what was his response?" Sam asked, finally sensing they were getting somewhere.

"He told me he was doing these people a favour. They seemed to be always too busy to see him during the day."

"And you believed him?"

"Did I heck. Like I've already said, the shutters came down years ago. He was the type who rarely, if ever, opened up. I don't think I ever saw the real him. At one point, I thought he was cheating on me because of his mood swings."

"How long were you together?"

"Fifteen years, give or take a few months. Most of them, especially the latter ones, were spent in misery."

"Sorry to hear that. I don't suppose your husband mentioned Pendle House, did he?"

Katy Weller paused to think and then shook her head. "No, I don't think he ever mentioned that name. Hang on, I do remember something, but I don't think it was because Stephen ever brought the subject up. Was it some kind of school?"

"Yes, it was shut down years ago, mainly because of an abuse scandal. We found a document that revealed Stephen was the planning officer who signed off the redevelopment of the site."

She clicked her fingers together. "Yes, that's right. I pass by the luxury flats that were erected in its place when I visit my mum in the care home. It's over on that side of town."

"Did he ever mention anything about that development?"

"No, nothing. He never discussed his work; he always told me that it would bore me rigid. I never pushed him on it because I assumed he was right."

"Do you know if he'd had any kind of trouble come his way in the last few months?"

"I'm so sorry, I really wouldn't know. He was the same every day, walking around as if he had troubles galore. I gave up asking in the end, only because he always gave me the same answer: that he was fine and there was nothing wrong. He usually stopped short of telling me to keep my nose out, although sometimes he threw that into the mix, too. It was awful, dealing with his attitude day in and day out. It wasn't a marriage; there was no intimacy, and we never spent any quality time together."

"What about holidays? Didn't you go away?"

"I did. With my friends. We never went anywhere as a couple."

"Did he go away?"

"Yes, he'd frequently go on short business trips. Again, he always kept me in the dark about what they were for. I got sick of asking, and that's when the hatred towards him crept into our relationship. I used to go out with friends and sit there, listening to them all praise their husbands for doing something nice for them. You know the type of thing, surprising them with a bunch of flowers or a weekend away somewhere. I had nothing like that in my life at all. In the end, it wore me down, and all I could think about was escaping my vile existence."

"Was he ever violent towards you?"

"No. He had no feelings towards me whatsoever; at least, that's the impression I got by the end of our relationship. That's when I put my foot down and told him I wanted a divorce. He refused to leave the house and told me if I wanted to move out, he would cover my expenses until the house was sold."

"So, you chose that option and ended up here?"

"Yes. I know it's not the best of places, but at least I feel safe here."

"More than you did at home? But you told us he wasn't violent towards you."

She let out a large sigh. "I know. The thought was always there, and I struggled to shift it. He was a hard man to read at the best of times, even more so when the red mist descended. Before I chose to end the marriage, the angry days were becoming more and more regular. I had to call it a day, if only for my own mental health. I was existing there, not living. If that makes sense?"

"It does. Do you have a job?"

"No. He didn't want me to work, and I was happy to go along with that, most of the time. Maybe it was the boredom that triggered me seeking the divorce. My friend has given me the option to start up in business with her. I'm mulling the offer over at the moment."

"What type of business?"

"A new beauty treatment that is coming over from America."

"Has she asked you to put any money into the business?" Sam asked, her mind wandering off in a different direction.

"Yes, but I've told her I won't be able to do that for several months, until I receive the money from the house sale. She's willing to wait, which I'm thrilled about." She fell quiet and looked down at her hands clenched in her lap. After a second or two, she glanced up and asked, "Does this mean I can move back into the house now?"

Sam shrugged. "I don't see why not. SOCO will have to examine the property for evidence over the next day or two."

"They will? Why?"

"Because your husband was murdered and we need to uncover the reason behind his death. There might be a clue in the house somewhere. Do you know if there was a safe there?"

"No, he had a small office. You should find all you need in there. I told him not to litter the house with his stuff. Of course, that might have all changed with me moving out of the house."

"We'll see. Is there anything else you'd like to add before we leave?"

She sniffled and shook her head. "Sorry, I'm not sure why I'm getting upset. It's not like I loved him."

"It's probably the shock setting in. Is there anyone we can call to come and sit with you?"

"No. I'll be fine. I'll pop to the shops; that'll keep my mind occupied. One more question, if I may?"

"Of course. What's that?"

"Did he suffer? I know that probably sounds a stupid question."

"No, it's an obvious one that we get most of the time. Given the extent of his injuries, I have to be honest with you and say it's hard to tell."

"I'm shocked to hear that. I know he wasn't the most caring of characters, but I wouldn't wish that sort of ending on him."

Sam and Bob rose from their seats.

She handed Katy one of her cards. "Give me a call if you think of anything else we should know. We'll see ourselves out." She didn't bother giving the woman her condolences, not after the conversation they'd just held.

"I will. I hope you find the person who killed him. Wait, I've just had a thought..."

Sam paused in the doorway. "What's that?"

"You don't think whoever killed him will come after me, do you?"

"No, I don't think so. Although it might be better to up your security at your flat, just for your peace of mind. I can see you have a chain on the door; it would make sense to use that before you open the door to strangers."

"Oh yes. I've never felt the need to use it before. I'll do that, thank you. What about the house?"

"I'll send your details over to SOCO now. A member of the team will be in touch with you soon."

"Okay. I'll wait to hear from them. Thank you."

Sam smiled and exited the flat with Bob.

"Are you all right?" he asked once they were ten feet away from the flat.

"What makes you ask?"

"You seemed a bit antsy towards her back there."

"Did I? I didn't mean to be. It's the way the conversation turned. At one point, I thought she might have been behind his murder. Until I reminded myself that this is the third murder we're dealing with during the investigation. Had he been the first victim we had discovered, she would definitely be high up on the suspect list."

"Wow, really? I didn't get that about her at all. Mind you, after the way he'd treated her over the years, who could blame her for wanting to bump him off? Some men need a good pasting and a lecture now and again about how to treat women properly."

Sam smiled. "You're a good man, Bob. Abigail is lucky to have you."

"You might want to tell her that; I think she has a tendency to forget now and again."

"I'll call her later."

He stopped on the stairs and hooked her arm. "No. You can't do that."

Sam doubled over with laughter. "As if I would. She'd likely crucify the pair of us."

"Phew, I thought you were being bloody serious then. A boss should never interfere in someone's marriage."

"For your information, I wouldn't dream of it." Sam winked and tapped the side of her nose. "Your secrets are safe with me, big man, never fear."

They continued on their journey.

"Why do I always feel uneasy when you say, 'never fear'?"

BACK IN THE CAR, Sam rang and organised the team. She also placed a call to the SOCO team to arrange picking up the key to Weller's house from his wife. She told them he had an office but couldn't tell them if there was a safe in the house or not. Then she and Bob drove to the council offices in Workington and followed the signs for the Planning Department. Sam showed her warrant card and introduced herself and Bob to the receptionist.

"We'd like to speak with whoever is in charge today."

"Ah, that would be Mrs Kilner. Our usual boss, Mr Weller, isn't here right now."

"Mrs Kilner will do, thanks."

The receptionist picked up her phone and turned her back on them to make the call. She hung up and said, "She won't be long. If you'd like to take a seat. Can I get you a drink?"

"We'll pass on that, thanks all the same."

Sam and Bob stepped back. Instead of sitting in the waiting area, they studied what was on the noticeboard. It highlighted several new developments in the area, which Sam recognised as being beneficial to the community.

"This one is close to where you live, isn't it?"

"Yep. Don't get me started on that. The local residents are up in arms about it."

"Why?"

Bob didn't get a chance to answer because a woman in a dark-grey suit appeared.

"Hello, I'm Mrs Kilner. I've been told you'd like a word with me."

"Yes, that's right. I'm DI Sam Cobbs, and this is my partner, DS Bob Jones. Would it be possible to speak with you in private?"

"That sounds ominous. Come through. Have you been offered a drink?"

"We have. We're fine at the moment."

She led the way up the corridor into a larger-than-average room. "I'm using our boss's office today. He's not shown up for work, and there was a lot of work that needed to be dealt with on his desk. It was easier to do it in here rather than ferry it all to my office across the way. Please, take a seat. What can I do for you today?"

Sam and Bob sat.

"Umm... it's to do with your boss that we've come here today."

Mrs Kilner frowned and sat upright in the executive chair. "Oh, can I ask what you mean by that?"

"Have you tried to contact him?"

"Yes, I've been trying on and off all morning. Why? Don't tell me something has happened to him? Damn, that thought never even crossed my mind. Is he okay? Should I call his wife? I know they're separated, but I'm sure she'd want to know if he's been in an accident."

Sam raised a hand to stop her from asking anything else. "Sorry to interrupt you. Mr Weller wasn't in any accident."

Mrs Kilner flopped back in her chair, relieved. "Thank goodness. So, where is he then, and why haven't I been able to contact him all morning?"

"I'm afraid Mr Weller's body was found this morning at a construction site."

She sprang forward in her seat and shook her head. "He what? I can't believe I heard that right. He's dead?"

"That's correct. I can't go into details as to how he died. What I need to know is why he was at the site. Do you know?"

"Me? How would I know?"

"Can you tell me if he was due to meet anyone at the location last night?"

"No. We rarely visit the locations once the planning application has been successful. What stage is the development in? Can you tell me?"

"The builders are on site. It's at the industrial unit on the other side of town."

"If it's the one I'm thinking about, there should be no reason he would have been there. I can check for you if you'll give me a moment."

"If you wouldn't mind, thank you."

She booted up the computer, which thankfully didn't take long to come to life, and typed in the information. "Here it is. Yes, it was all signed off on our part, and that should have been the end of our involvement. Oh my, I wonder what he was doing there."

"That's what we're trying to find out. Can you tell us when you last saw him?"

"He was still in the office when the rest of us left at five-thirty last night. I dropped in here to ask him if he was going to be long. He assured me he had some paperwork to finish and that he'd be leaving within the next fifteen minutes. My colleagues and I left him to it. Gone are the days I offer to stay behind and help out."

Sam frowned. "What makes you say that?"

"Because I've offered to assist him several times in the past, only to be told that he didn't need my help. I'm the same with everyone, eager to assist them if it makes their lives easier. That's what people do when they're part of a team, isn't it?"

"Yes, you're right. But he always turned down your offer to lend a hand. Did he say why?"

"Just that he preferred to do things on his own."

"Did he stay behind a lot?"

Mrs Kilner nodded slowly. "Now that you mention it, yes, he did, more so than anyone else in the department."

"Isn't that what bosses tend to do in general, though?"

"They might do elsewhere, but not around here, not in my experience. Damn, I still can't believe he's dead and that this could be work-related."

"Sorry if I gave you that impression. As yet, we don't know if that's a fact or not. Our investigation is still in the preliminary stages. One thing that has come to our attention is a possible link to Pendle House."

"Wow, there's a name I haven't heard in a long time. I believe Stephen was the officer who assisted the developer in obtaining the correct planning permission, back in the day."

"I don't suppose you can let us have a look at the file, can you?"

"I'm sorry, not without a warrant. As you can appreciate, the files are treated as confidential."

Sam smiled. "It was worth a try. Maybe you can tell us what time Stephen left last night, then? I'm assuming you have an alarm system here that is set every night."

Mrs Kilner lifted a finger and nodded. "Of course. I can get that information for you." She pounded the keyboard and turned the screen to face Sam and Bob. "This is the information for this week, and for last night in particular. He left at precisely six forty-three and set the alarm behind him."

"Perhaps you can tell us if he had any meetings planned for after work?"

"I don't think so. He had quite a busy schedule yesterday as it was."

"Can you check for us?"

She opened another file, and Sam watched her eyebrows shoot up into her fringe.

"This is interesting."

Sam shuffled forward to the edge of her seat and squinted at the screen. "What am I looking at?"

"Here." Mrs Kilner pointed at the relevant information. "It states that he had a meeting with 'I' at seven-thirty."

Sam and Bob glanced at each other.

"But it doesn't tell us where the meeting was due to take place," Sam said.

"No, that's all it says."

"I... Any idea who that could be?"

Mrs Kilner flicked back a few pages to the weekly schedule on the screen. "I can't see anything here. For all we know, it could be anyone."

"It's a start and helps us understand that he met someone last night, possibly connected with work, if it was entered on his work schedule."

"So it would seem. I'm sorry I can't be of any more help. It's frustrating, isn't it? Knowing he's met someone and that person more than likely killed him."

"I agree. Has anyone visited him lately who didn't fit well with you or your staff in the office?"

"I don't understand your question, sorry."

"Has someone visited the department and had an argument with

Stephen, or did you notice if he seemed awkward during or just after a visit?"

"Nothing that I can recall. I'm telling you, all this has come as a total shock to me. He was a strange man. I'm not the only one to think that. None of the staff ever felt as though they could relax in his presence."

"That's interesting to know. You think he was open to taking back-handers?"

"God, I hope not. I don't think so, but who can tell these days? We often get accused of it if decisions don't go the public's way."

"I can imagine. Okay, I can't think of anything else right now. I'll go back to the station and get the warrant ordered."

"I'm sorry I couldn't be of more help in that respect."

"Don't worry, I quite understand. If you wouldn't mind asking around to see if any of your team noticed anything out of the ordinary with Mr Wellen in recent months, I'd appreciate it."

"Of course." She stood and held the door open for them. "Fingers crossed you find out who did this to our boss soon." She showed them back to the reception area.

Sam and Bob left the building.

Sam paused outside to suck in a lungful of air. "Well, that was a waste of time, wasn't it?"

"Do you think there was anything suspicious in what she told us?"

"I'm not getting that impression, are you?"

"No. I wondered if I had missed something, so I thought I'd better check."

"I don't think so. Right, let's get back to the station." During the journey back, Sam's head was full of questions, some more obvious than others, which went a long way to up her frustration levels. "I can't put it off any longer," she said as she drew into her parking space.

"Huh? I'm not with you. What are you talking about?"

She stared at the brick wall of the station ahead of her, still gripping the steering wheel tightly. "I need to see what Rhys knows about Pendle House."

"That'll make an interesting conversation over dinner this evening. I wouldn't mind being a fly on the wall for that."

She faced him and replied, "No, I don't think I should put it off any longer. I'm going to call him and see if he'll either come to the station or meet me somewhere for a coffee."

"Ah, that makes sense. I would have thought neutral ground would be better; otherwise, you're going to put the wind up him by requesting that he meets you here, at the station."

"Possibly. I'll weigh up the pros and cons over the next half an hour. It might be wiser to leave it until we've seen if the rest of the team have found anything else in that file during our absence."

"I agree. God, I don't envy you having to tackle your partner about something that happened in his past."

"I can't say I'm relishing it. That's why I've put it off for so long."

AFTER THE OTHER team members arrived, Sam checked with them. Although they had discovered further details about Pendle, none of them had spotted anything else regarding Rhys, which came as a relief to Sam. However, it didn't alter the fact that she needed to see him and delve a little deeper. She left Bob to deal with the request for the warrant while she went through to her office to make the call in private. She paused to look at the view of the hills on the way to her desk. It usually helped to alleviate any anger within her, but not this time. Once she'd settled into her chair and she had the phone in her hand, beads of sweat broke out above her upper lip.

Bugger, how do I word this? I've barely spoken to him in the last twenty-four hours, and now here I am, about to summon him to the station. No, I can't do it. It's going to have to be somewhere else.

After drawing in a couple of deep breaths and letting them out slowly to calm her nerves, she made the call. Rhys's secretary answered the phone promptly, much quicker than she'd anticipated.

"Oh, hi, Brenda. It's Sam. I don't suppose Rhys is free at the moment, is he?"

"As it happens, he is. His next appointment isn't for a few hours. He told me he was intending to catch up on some paperwork."

"Ah, okay. Would you mind putting me through so I can have a brief chat with him?"

"Of course, Sam. Hold the line."

There was a pause, during which Sam struggled to prevent her heart from racing. She opened the drawer and removed a fresh bottle of water. She held the phone between her ear and shoulder to open it.

"I'm back. I'll pass you through now, Sam."

"Thanks, Brenda. I shouldn't keep him too long."

"No worries. I bet you're getting excited about the wedding now. You must be, what with it only being a few weeks away."

"We are. Did he give you your invite?"

"He did. I'm looking forward to it. I've even splashed out and bought myself a new dress and fascinator for the occasion."

"Wow, you really shouldn't have spent out like that."

"Don't be silly. It's not every day your boss gets married."

Sam laughed. "I hope that's the case."

"See you soon, Sam. I'm connecting you now."

The phone rang a couple of times before Rhys answered, making Sam even more jittery than she was already. She had a dreaded fear that he wouldn't want to speak to her.

If that were the case, he would have told Brenda to tell me he was busy. He didn't, so there's no reason for him not to take my call.

"Hi, this is a nice surprise. What's up, Sam?"

"Umm... hi. Thanks for accepting my call. Are you free to meet me for a quick coffee?"

"What? Wow, I don't think you've ever asked me to meet you during the day before. Hang on, is there something wrong?" he asked, a note of apprehension surfacing in his tone.

"No, not really. Can you meet me or not?" she asked, sharper than she'd intended.

"Is it going to be one of those kinds of meetings where you shout at me all the time? If so, I'd rather give it a miss, if it's all the same to you."

"Sorry. No, I promise, it's not. Although, I do have something important I need to discuss with you."

"Something important? Shit, you're not going to call the wedding off, are you?"

"Rhys, don't be so ridiculous. Where do you want to meet? The sooner, the better for me. Brenda said your diary is clear for the next few hours."

"She's a traitor. There's no way I can back out of a meeting now, is there? What about the café around the corner from my office? Or is that too far for you to come?"

"No, that will be ideal. I'll see you there in ten to fifteen minutes, depending on the traffic."

"I'll see you then, darling."

Sam welled up. She whispered goodbye, then replaced the phone in its docking station. She glanced up to see Bob standing in the doorway, watching her. "Don't say a word."

He smiled. "Don't be too hard on him, Sam."

She rose from her seat and walked towards him. "I know you think I'm being silly."

"You are."

"It's the deceit I'm struggling to handle. I had to deal with it for so many years with Chris. It changes you, Bob. Don't forget, I'm also dealing with what Claire has done to me, to all of us, on top of everything else."

"I admit, none of this is easy. All I'm saying is don't go into the meeting screaming at him. He doesn't deserve that."

"I know. I'll take your well-meaning advice on board."

"Good, because that's what it is. I'm only looking out for you."

She smiled and rubbed his arm. "I know and I appreciate it. I shouldn't be too long."

"You know where I am if you need me. Talking of which, is there anything specific you'd like me to do in your absence? And yes, the request has already gone in for the warrant."

"In that case, can you keep sifting through the file with the rest of the team?"

"I was going to do that anyway. Do you want me to call the lab to see if they've got anything for us yet?"

"Why not? It wouldn't hurt to keep them on their toes with this one, especially considering how quickly the murders are happening. The killer has an agenda, and we don't know where or when they are going to strike next."

"Exactly. Okay, leave it with me. Drive carefully and try not to be too harsh on your future husband when you get there."

She mock-saluted him. "I'll let you know when I'm on my way back."

SAM DROVE to the location and parked up in the square opposite the café. She crossed the road. Rhys was already there, sitting at a table next to the window. They waved at each other. Bile burned the back of her throat the closer she got to the entrance of the café.

I guess an afternoon cream cake is out of the question. I doubt if I would keep it down.

The girl standing behind the till welcomed her with a smile. "Can I help you?"

Sam returned the smile and pointed at Rhys. "My fiancé is already here." She was pleased to hear, to her credit, that she didn't stumble over the word fiancé.

"Ah, okay. Do you know what you want?"

"A flat white would be perfect. Thanks."

"I can't tempt you with a cake?"

"Believe me, I'm very tempted, but I'm getting married in a few weeks, so I need to watch my waistline."

"Oh, how wonderful. Congratulations, and yes, cream cakes would be off the menu for me too if I were in your shoes. I'll bring your coffee over when it's ready."

"Thanks very much." Sam paid for the drink and then weaved her way through the tables, some full and others empty after the lunchtime rush.

Rhys stood and held out her chair for her.

"A bit over the top given the setting," she said.

"You're worth all the sniggers and whisperings coming my way from the customers." He bent and pecked her on the cheek, then sat and laid his hand upwards on the table, ready to accept hers.

Sam hesitated for a moment or two, then decided against it. "Sorry, I need to keep my professional head on."

Rhys shrugged and seemed hurt by the rejection. He withdrew his hand as the waitress arrived with Sam's coffee.

"Enjoy," she said, then left them to it.

"What's this about, Sam? Last night you barely said two words to me, and today you won't even hold hands with me in public. What gives?"

"I won't hold hands because I'm here on police business, and it wouldn't feel right to show you affection."

"Police business? I don't understand. Does this have anything to do with the bastard who knifed me? Don't tell me he's escaped from prison?"

"He hasn't, and no, it doesn't have anything to do with you getting attacked." She opened two sachets of sugar and poured them into her cup. "This is hard for me to say; I've been trying to summon up the words since yesterday."

He frowned. "You're getting me worried now. Just say it. If it comes out wrong, we'll sort it out later."

Sam gripped her cup with both hands as their gazes met. She could see the torture she was causing deep within his eyes. "It's to do with the investigation we're dealing with at the moment."

"Go on. Sam, just say what's on your mind and stop dragging it out, will you?"

"I'm sorry. You have no idea what this information is doing to me."

He fell back in his chair and ran a hand through his short hair. "I can't help you if you won't tell me what you're going on about."

She exhaled and took a sip from her coffee, prolonging his agony but, at the same time, ensuring the words she was about to say came out in the correct order.

"Sam?" He shook his head and stared at her.

She could tell his patience was waning rapidly.

"All right. Here goes. In the past few days, as you know, we've had to deal with two murders, one being that of a member of my team." She glanced over her shoulder, aware of the other customers sitting at the nearest tables, and lowered her voice. "The thing is, this morning we were called out to another crime scene..."

"My God. Are they all connected? If so, how do you know they are?"

"Yes, we believe we're dealing with the same killer because they keep leaving us messages, mostly, maybe all of them, written in the victims' blood."

"Jesus, even Claire's murder?"

"I think so, or maybe it was spray paint; I can't honestly remember, and that in itself is a worrying sign for me. Anyway, when we showed up to assess Claire's murder, we found a USB stick with some vital information on it about a certain... children's home in the area." She paused to consider his reaction. "Anyhow, this USB led us to the other victims and has also given us further insight into..."

"Into what? None of this is making any sense to me. What am I missing, and why does this concern me?"

"Does the name Pendle House mean anything to you?"

He sprang forward and gripped his cup tightly. "Yes, of course it does. I did some of my training there. It wasn't long, only two or three weeks, but... hang on a minute, what are you saying? That you think I have something to do with the murders?"

"I'm not suggesting anything of the sort. Why didn't you tell me you worked there or had a placement there?"

"What? Why should I? I had dozens of placements throughout the country during my time at university. It's what they used to do back in the day. I think the system has changed now. I still don't understand how this could cause an issue between us. Care to explain?"

Sam covered her face with her hands, shook her head, then released her hands when she thought she'd sorted through her thoughts enough to make any sense. "It's the lies, the deceit; it's coming at me from all sides, and I've struggled to handle it. You know what I went through with Chris."

"Excuse me! I'm nothing like him and, for your information, I don't think I've ever consciously lied to you since I've known you. Why are you punishing me for something that is out of my hands? For something that happened decades ago, just because you saw my name on a file of *employees*? I can't believe this, Sam. I thought you knew me better than this. The question is, do you believe me?"

Sam turned her cup in her saucer and remained silent until he spoke again.

"Clearly not. What the actual...? What did I do wrong? I worked in a placement at a children's home, which, years later, gained a despicable reputation. I repeat, in case you misheard me, long after I 'worked' there, and you're sitting here now, what? Blaming me for being associated with the place? How is that even possible?"

She took a sip from her coffee and glanced out of the window. "I'm sorry. With what I've had to deal with this week, I kind of let things get on top of me."

"What things? Claire betraying you? Is that what you're alluding to? What does that have to do with me? None of this is making any sense, no matter which way I try to interpret it."

"Tell me about it. If you want to call the wedding off because of the way I've treated you, I quite understand."

He stared at his cup and scratched his head. "I'm going to need to seriously consider what our relationship means to me because, from what you've just said, you seem undecided about whether you can trust me." He pushed back his chair and left the table.

Sam was mortified that he would choose to walk out on her, but after a moment's reflection, she shrugged.

Who can blame him? I've treated him no better than a common criminal and blamed him for something that he apparently had no control over.

The waitress appeared like a fairy godmother beside her. "Sorry to intrude. You seem upset. Is everything all right?"

"I don't know. Thanks for the coffee; it was lovely. Although I'm surprised it didn't choke me." She stood and pushed her chair under the table.

"Please don't leave like this. You're obviously upset. I'd hate it if you got in your car and had an accident."

"Don't worry about me. I've had to deal with more than a relationship breakup in the past."

"What? But you're supposed to be getting married. Didn't you say he was your fiancé?"

"He was. I don't know if he still is, not after this. I guess I'll find out the answer to that when I go home this evening."

"How sad. Wishing you all the best. Perhaps it's a case of wedding day jitters."

Sam smiled. "If only that were true. Thank you for caring."

"I hope your day gets better for you."

"Christ, it can't get any worse."

Sam smiled again and weaved her way back through the tables to the front door. She peered down the street and spotted Rhys marching towards his office, his head bowed low and his shoulders slumped in resignation. Sam's heart went out to him. She cursed herself for overreacting and causing a rift in their relationship.

I'll be lucky if it is a rift. I'm fearing the worst—that this might be the end of us.

She crossed the street, got back in the car, and even thought about chasing after Rhys, but the second she set off, she changed her mind.

Sam didn't have time to dwell on it. Her phone rang, and Bob's name showed up on the screen. "I'm on my way back. I should be about ten minutes. What's up?"

"Good. You can pick me up. We've got another body."

"Shit! I'll be there soon." She ended the call and slammed her flattened hand against the steering wheel.

Haven't we got enough? Give me a lead that will bring me face to face with you, at least, you bastard!

6

A t the scene, Sam struggled to figure out how a doctor could be found dead in his consulting room halfway through the day. She asked for clarification from the receptionist.

"I was asked to cancel all his appointments until this afternoon. He also told me to come in late today as I wouldn't be needed."

Sam glanced around the empty waiting room. The second surgery she'd visited this week, both empty, and yet there was outcry from the general public about the need to sit on the phone every morning in the hope of being offered an appointment. The new system was a sham, a disgrace to society, especially if this was the result.

"I see. What time did you arrive?"

"Just after two. I saw Dr Trigg's car was out the back, and when I came in, his door was closed. I presumed he didn't want to be disturbed and that he was either catching up on paperwork or on a call to a patient."

"What time did you find him?"

"It was a good half an hour later, so around two-thirty, give or take." She sniffled and wiped her nose. Tears dripped onto her cheek.

"I'm sorry. I'm trying my best to hold it together. It's not easy, not after seeing him like that. It was such a shock."

"I'm sure it was. Are you alone here?"

"Yes. I'm the receptionist, and Dr Trigg is—or should I say *was*—the only doctor on duty this week. The other two doctors are on holiday and maternity leave. Jesus, why would someone kill him, let alone bloody do that to him? I don't get it. You see and hear about horrendous crimes like this on the TV all the time. I never thought I'd have to deal with it personally, though. It's just shocking."

"I know. I'm sorry you were the one who discovered the body. Why don't you take a seat, and I'll make you a drink?"

The receptionist waved the suggestion away. "It's fine. I only drink water. I'm on a diet; I've lost three stone since January."

"That's incredible. Well done. Before we get in there and assess the scene, is there anything you can tell us about Dr Trigg? By that I mean, has he had any problems lately that you're aware of, either at work or at home? Is he married? That should have been my first question."

"No. He got divorced last year. His wife moved away with their two children. She now lives in Kent, I believe. Dr Trigg went down to see them last month, knowing that he wouldn't be able to visit them again until Christmas because of what's going on around here with the other two doctors."

"I don't suppose you have the ex-wife's address, do you?"

"No. I would have no need to know that. As for anything else going on in Dr Trigg's life, I really wouldn't know. He didn't tend to confide in me that much. I don't think he was dating anyone else; he was not the type. I got the impression he was enjoying the peace and quiet at home. Some people suffer from depression after they get divorced. He hasn't, not that I've been aware of. But... oh God, you need to see him. Someone evil did this to him." Her hand trembled. "I can't believe what I saw in there. I screamed when I opened the door and took a step back. I thought I was going to pass out."

"You didn't enter the room?"

"No. I wanted to stay as far away from him as possible. I know that sounds awful, and I should have checked for a pulse, but his eyes were... it was obvious he was dead. What kind of sick piece of shit does something like this to a doctor?"

"We're going to find out who did this, I promise you. We'll need to get a statement from you; are you willing to do that now?"

"Yes. I'd like to get it over and done with. I think it would be therapeutic to get it out of my system; otherwise, I'm only going to dwell on it, let it fester, and what good is that going to do me?"

"Exactly. Have you cancelled all the appointments for today?"

"Yes, I dropped into professional mode after I rang 999 to report his death."

"That's great. Thank you for doing that." Sam peered over her shoulder at the two uniformed officers standing by the door. She recognised one of them. "It's Ray, isn't it?"

The taller officer beamed and took a step towards her. "That's right, ma'am. What can I do to help?"

She faced the receptionist again and asked, "I apologise. I didn't get your name."

"It's Hazel."

"Ray, I need you to sit down with Hazel and take a statement from her, if you will."

"With pleasure. I'll nip out to the car and get the paperwork, ma'am."

"I'll leave you in the constable's capable hands."

"Thank you." Hazel returned to sit behind the reception desk, her gaze drawn to the doctor's office.

Calmly professional, Sam joined Bob, who had collected two protective suits from the car. "I guessed we'd be needing these."

"I've received a message from Des. He's stuck in traffic on the other side of Workington. He should be with us soon."

"Nothing new. The traffic has been worse than abysmal lately. I'm surprised we didn't get caught in it."

"I think that's more down to my expert driving and knowledge of all the shortcuts in the area."

Bob snorted and rolled his eyes. "You keep telling yourself that.

Anyway, it gives us a chance to have a look in there. Did you get anything from the receptionist?"

"Nothing much. The victim is recently divorced. Let's change and get in there to see for ourselves what's going on. From what she's told me, I'm already inclined to link his death to the other murders."

"Without seeing him?"

Sam nodded. Once they were suited and booted, she placed her hand on the doorknob. "Brace yourself."

He nodded and lowered his voice so only Sam could hear what he had to say. "I'm fully braced and ready for anything this fucker is prepared to throw at us."

"You and me both." She opened the door and froze. "What the...? I forgot to ask, do you recognise his name?"

"Yep, from the list. Another reason we should suspect it's the same killer."

They stood in the doorway. Sam's gaze trained on the doctor. His hands were clasped in prayer over his chest, and his lips and eyes had been sewn shut, reminiscent of what had happened to the other victims, or some of them. She noticed there was a book open on the desk in front of him. They entered the room, and Sam immediately went to investigate what type of book it was, presuming it to be a medical reference book. Instead, she discovered it was the Bible. One passage in particular had been underlined in red:

FOR NOTHING IS HIDDEN **that will not be made manifest, nor is anything secret that will not be known and come to light.** Luke 8:17

"WHAT DOES THAT MEAN?" Bob said, reading it over her shoulder.

"I'm taking it to be a message from the killer about the victims and the part they've played in his or her past."

"Er, that much I kind of worked out for myself. The killer must be a warped fucker, that's all I can say."

"That's twice you've called them that today. Give me a break and don't say it a third time."

"That told me." Bob circled the room and stopped in front of the corkboard. "Shit!"

Intrigued, Sam approached him to see what he'd found. "What is it?"

"An old photo."

"I can see that. Who are all these people?"

The photo was yellowed and worn. Its edges curled with time.

Bob unpinned it and read what was written on the back. "Shit! It's a staff photo from Pendle House."

Sam peered closer at a specific person she thought she recognised —it was Rhys.

Bob did the same and tutted. "Is that Rhys?"

Sam's heart thundered until it made her gasp for breath, enough to worry her partner.

"Are you all right?"

She inhaled and exhaled a couple of deep breaths. "Look at his expression. It's haunting. His eyes are distant, wary almost. Or is that my imagination?"

"No, I'd call that a spot-on assessment. What is going on?"

"I don't know. I'm sensing he knows more about what went on at that children's home than he's willing to share with me."

"By what you told me in the car about your meeting earlier, I would have to agree. If that's the case, Sam, he's playing a dangerous game."

She paused, torn between the case and her relationship, not that she had the chance to consider that for long because Des and his team arrived.

"What have we got here, then?"

"Another doctor, and yes, we believe the cases are connected."

Des took one look at the victim and nodded. "I'd agree with your assessment. What do we know about him? And what are you holding, Inspector?"

"We've just found this photo pinned to the corkboard." She handed it to him.

"What am I looking at?"

"A staff photo from Pendle House."

"I take it the victim is on here?"

"I haven't got that far. We've only just discovered it." Sam compared the people in the photo to the victim, with Bob peering over her shoulder. "The names are handwritten on the back."

"Hang on, isn't that him?" Bob pointed to a young man at the rear. He was standing two feet away from Rhys.

Her gaze was drawn back to her fiancé.

"Do you agree?" Bob prompted.

"Yes, that's him. I wonder if the receptionist will give us a copy of this."

"I'll ask."

"Make sure she doesn't touch it. You deal with it and let her press the button. Not teaching you how to suck eggs or anything."

Bob grinned and left the room.

"Are you all right, Sam? You seem to be a little distracted during this investigation. Tell me to butt out if you have something personal going on at home."

"You're right. There is something. I'm just not sure how relevant it is right now."

"Are you going to let me in on this secret?"

Sam swallowed hard. "One of the people in that photo is Rhys."

"Whoa! As in your fella Rhys?"

"As in my bloody fiancé Rhys."

"Ouch! And what's he said about what's happened this week?"

"I met him about an hour ago to tackle him about it..."

"I take it things didn't go too well."

"No, he ended up walking away from me."

"That was mature of him. Have you told him he might be in danger? Correction, judging by the victim count already, I'd say that was a certainty."

"Don't say that. I didn't get around to telling him. Now that the killer has left the photo, it has just dawned on me the kind of danger he could be in."

"What are you waiting for then, Sam? You have to put aside the fact that you've fallen out and get over there... before it's too late."

Her pulse raced. "You're right. I'm sorry to run out on you like this."

He shooed her out of the office. "Go. I'll handle this side of things."

Bob approached them, perplexed. "What's going on?" He puffed out his chest and took a step towards Des. "Have you said something to upset her?"

Des tutted. "Calm down, Macho Man. Sam will explain en route."

Sam turned and smiled at Des, then sighed. "Thanks for your support. We're out of here." She ran through the reception area and out to the car, stopping only to remove her protective suit and dump it in the awaiting black sack. She rang Rhys's number. The phone rang and rang. She sighed, assuming that he's still cross with her after their meeting at the café.

"Christ, I wish I knew what was going on. Since when do you leave a crime scene two minutes after arriving?" Bob queried as he removed his suit.

"Since I realised that Rhys's life could be in imminent danger... again."

"Okay, that's a good enough reason."

SAM DROVE under the blues and twos and screeched to a halt outside Rhys's office. She and Bob raced into the building. Brenda placed a hand over her heart when they barged into the room.

"Sam? What's going on?"

"Is Rhys here?"

"No. I thought he was on his way to meet you. That's what he told me."

"We met, but I left him around forty minutes ago. Shit, where is he?" She removed her mobile from her pocket and punched in a single number. Rhys's phone rang and rang, but either he refused to answer it or was unable to. "Brenda, he might be ignoring my calls. Can you ring him?"

"Why would he do that?" Brenda asked as she dialled Rhys's number. She put it on speaker phone. It rang out again.

"I'm not liking this one bit," Sam said.

Bob withdrew his phone. "I'll get on to the station and put an alert out for him. Don't worry, Sam, we'll find him."

Sam paced back and forth until Bob finished his call. "Well?"

"Jason is on it now. He's alerted all patrols to be on the lookout for him."

"And the last you heard or saw of him was when he left the office on the way to meet me?"

Brenda nodded. "Yes. Oh, Sam, what does this mean?"

"I don't know. What I do know is that we can't just hang around here waiting for him to come back." She handed Brenda a business card. "Ring me if he contacts you."

"I will."

Brenda was still talking, but Sam needed to get on the road. As they reached the street, Bob latched on to her arm.

"Wait, you're not thinking straight. Give me your keys. I'm not prepared to let you drive when you're in this state."

"Fine. Take them." She threw the keys at him with force and then apologised. "We need to take the route he would have taken to meet me."

"He was on foot, wasn't he?"

"Yes."

They got in the car. Bob groaned and adjusted the seat to accommodate his longer legs. "I reckon we're gonna be wasting our time. He's probably taken the shortcut through the park."

Sam placed a hand on her cheek and shook her head as the realisation dawned. "Shit, yes, you're right. I never thought about that." Sam tutted, her eyes darting to every passerby as they sped through town. "Where the fuck is he?"

"I know you're not going to want to hear my suggestion, which is the obvious one."

"No, I don't. I'm trying not to think about it."

They both fell silent and continued the search. Before long, they drew up outside the café. Sam threw open her car door and went inside.

"Sorry to trouble you. I was in here earlier."

"Yes, I remember. Did you forget something?" the waitress asked.

"The man I was with... did he come back after I left?"

"No, at least I don't think he did. Can't you find him?"

Sam's lip trembled, and she swallowed down the emotion that had surfaced in her throat. "He's gone missing, and he's not answering his phone."

"I'm sorry to hear that. If he comes back, I'll tell him you're looking for him. My fella is the same after we've had an argument. He always denies the phone ringing at his end. I'm sure things will turn out for the best later."

Sam smiled and backed out of the café.

I'm not. I'm a police officer, working a serial killer investigation, and I think the killer has targeted my fiancé. How I don't want to consider the ins and outs of my theory. But I know in my heart that something bad has happened to him.

She shook her head, trying to rid her mind of such a disturbing thought.

"Any news?" Bob asked, springing up from behind her.

"Do you have to bloody creep up on me like that?"

He grinned. "Your problem is that you're too jumpy."

"May I remind you why? It looks like my fiancé has been abducted."

Bob raised his hands. "All right. There's no need to chew my balls off."

Sam marched back to the car and muttered, "Do you even have a pair?"

"I heard that," he shouted from behind. "Hey, I'm driving."

Sam slammed the driver's door shut, which she'd opened out of habit, and flew round the other side of the car.

"Where do you want to go now?" Bob asked.

"Back to the station. It's pointless us being out here, unless you've got any suggestions?"

"I haven't."

He started the engine and headed back to the station, but veered off at the last minute.

"This isn't the way. What are you doing?"

"We're close to the lab. I thought we'd drop in and see if they can improve the photo for us. Is that all right?"

"Yep, okay. That makes sense. Make it quick, though."

He tutted and pressed his foot down on the accelerator. "Quick enough for you?"

"Hey, remember whose car this is."

"As if I'm likely to forget."

THEY ARRIVED BACK at the station an hour later with the improved image.

"Any news yet?" Sam asked the desk sergeant as soon as she entered the reception area.

He seemed very down in the mouth, not like his usual cheery self at all. "I wish there was, ma'am. I'll keep on top of my lads and make sure they continue their search for the rest of the day and beyond if necessary."

"Let's hope there's no need for that. Thanks, Jason."

Bob entered his code, and the security door sprang open. The team all glanced up when they entered the room.

Sam immediately raised a hand to stop them from offering her any sympathy. "I appreciate what you're about to say, but guys, I don't want to hear it. What I want, no, what I *need*, is for us to concentrate fully on this investigation. If the killer has Rhys, which is looking more and more likely, we need to find out who this person is... I'm sensing his life is in mortal danger." She choked up.

Her gaze met Bob's. His smile encouraged her to finish her speech.

She coughed to clear her throat and forced her shoulders back. "Bob, can you do the honours of showing the team what we found at the latest murder scene?"

Bob removed the copy of the photo the lab had enhanced and handed it around to the team. The faces of the people were much clearer now, and it didn't take Liam long to recognise someone.

"Umm... isn't that Claire at the back? I might be wrong, but it definitely looks like her."

"Have you got the original copy, Bob? It had the names on the back."

He removed it from the file. It was still in the evidence bag, so he turned it over. "What was Claire's maiden name? Do we know?"

"I'm not sure. I can check her personnel file. Just see if there's a Claire on the back row for now."

Bob took his time sourcing the information. "Yes, I've got a Claire Holden here."

Sam rushed over to a spare computer, switched it on, punched in her password and opened up the personnel folder. There it was, Claire Holden. "Yep, that's her. Shit, I can't believe she was more involved in this than we thought."

"Bugger. And we thought we knew her," Bob said, shaking his head.

"Exactly. Let me see the photo again." Something was bugging Sam about what she was looking at.

Bob moved to stand beside her. "What are you thinking?"

"That not all these people are staff. Is Claire wearing a uniform? A few of the other kids are dressed the same."

Liam handed Bob a magnifying glass that he kept in his drawer. "This might help."

"Bloody hell, it does, thanks, Liam. You're right. Would kids wear uniforms in a children's home? Did they, back in the day?"

Sam shook her head, perched on the desk behind her and puffed out her cheeks. "I don't know. Maybe they were older kids, perhaps volunteers who attended a nearby school. It's something we need to clarify." She jumped up and searched the personnel file again. "It says here that she attended St Mark's School. There's nothing in her CV that suggests she lived at Pendle House."

"Maybe you're right, then. It might be worth checking with Scott, or perhaps with her parents, if they're still around."

Sam grimaced. "The timing isn't right, not when they're dealing with her death and probably busy making the funeral arrangements. Let's put that to one side for now. We can revisit it later. We've got all we need to know: that she was definitely linked to Pendle House, just like the other victims and, apparently, Rhys." She paused to fill her lungs with more air. "It's obvious all the victims knew something about the house, a secret of sorts. We need to find out what it was. Remind me when the abuse rumours started to circulate about that place?"

Oliver searched his notes and shook his head. "I don't think that can be it. They didn't start until a few years later, boss."

"That's not to say the abuse wasn't going on long before that, though," Bob pitched in.

"That's true. If only Rhys had been more open with me about his experience."

"None of us could have foreseen this happening," Bob said.

"Claire knew something; maybe we'll find the answer on her computer," Liam suggested.

"Or maybe in her drawers," Sam added.

Bob raised his eyebrows.

She punched him in the arm. "I meant in her desk."

"Thanks for the clarification. It's always good to have."

Sam stared at the computer screen. "She wasn't just a detective," she said quietly. "She was trying to uncover her past, and now it's coming for the rest of us."

"What? You can't possibly believe that's true, Sam," Bob said, appalled by her revelation.

"Can't I? As far as we know, the killer has already abducted Rhys. He might be dead by now... Just another victim waiting to be discovered. How many more are out there?" She tapped a finger on the photo. "We've got to make it our priority to warn all the others in this photo."

Bob sighed. "What if one of them is the killer?"

OVER THE NEXT couple of hours, the team knuckled down and managed to contact most of the people in the photo. They were warned to remain vigilant at all times. While the team were dishing out the warnings, they also enquired if the people knew why they might be specifically targeted. The reply, across the board, had been a resounding "I don't know."

Sam had spent the time in her office completing some important paperwork, which acted as a distraction to stop her worrying about Rhys. Most of the time, it had worked, too. But every now and again, Sam's attention was drawn back to the photo lying on the desk beside her, like a splinter of betrayal. Claire, someone she'd trusted with her life for years, had lied, not only to her but to the whole team. She'd kept an entire piece of her life hidden. Sam felt torn; she didn't know whether to feel angry, heartbroken, or foolish. Her head was a mess, and then, on top of all this, she had Rhys's disappearance prodding her like a stick.

She picked up her phone and dialled his number. She held her breath while it rang out, until the voicemail clicked in, and out of curiosity she listened to it, just in case the kidnapper had decided to alter the message Rhys had uploaded. Her fiancé's voice calmed her, but the anger soon returned.

Her roller-coaster ride of emotions had taken its toll on her today, and now, at the end of their shift, she was going to be forced to go home and deal with the dogs.

Shit! Casper, he's still at the office with Brenda.

She gave the secretary a call. "Brenda, I'm so sorry for running out on you the way I did earlier. I totally forgot about Casper. I'll come and pick him up."

"Sam, you've got enough on your plate. He's fine with me. Let me take him home this evening."

"What? Are you sure?"

"It would be a pleasure. Terry and I can take him for a walk and pick up some dog food when we get home. He seems settled here."

"What would we do without you? If you're sure you don't mind?"

"I've already run it past Terry, and he's up for it. We lost our Max a year ago and have been considering whether to get another dog or not. Rhys keeps telling me how special Tilly is; we think we're going to rescue a pup, just like you have. This might be the push we need to see if we're up for it."

"I can put you in touch with the organisation I used, no problem."

"Let's see how the dog sitting goes for now."

"I'll call you later this evening if that's all right?"

Brenda gave Sam her mobile number and ended the call.

Sam felt relieved she only had Tilly to deal with later. Doreen was going to be shocked to hear the news about Rhys.

Her thoughts drifted back to Claire. It was a struggle for her to get past the deceit. She had always prided herself on being able to read people and on knowing who to trust.

Now... that confidence was crumbling fast.

First Claire. Now Rhys. How many more secrets were buried just beneath the surface?

Bob pushed the door open with his foot. He entered the room carrying two mugs of coffee. He paused when he saw her tortured expression. "Shit! Are you okay?"

"No," she admitted, her voice brittle. "I'm struggling to get past the fact that Claire showed up for work every day and deceived me for years. At least, that's how it feels."

Bob put the mug in front of her and sat.

"I gave her my trust. Shared intimate details with her. Now I'm sitting here wondering if I ever really knew her at all. What the fuck, Bob? I trust all of you and treat you all as if you were my family. Am I wrong to do that?"

"Without knowing the truth, we don't know her reasons for

keeping that side of her life from you, from all of us. Let's face it, Sam, it's not only you who feels betrayed. There's a sombre atmosphere out there. This has affected the team, all of us, even Nick."

"I know. I don't really want to make this all about me." She rubbed her temples. "What does this truly say about me? About my instincts? I missed it all. I keep missing it. First Claire, now Rhys... What if I can't trust anyone anymore?"

Bob hesitated. No wisecracks forthcoming—only one question, straight from his heart: "Do you trust me?"

She glanced up, her eyes stinging. "Yes, I think so." But even as she said it, a sliver of doubt remained. For the first time in her career, Sam wondered if the cost of uncovering the truth might be more than she could bear. Her gaze drifted towards the photo again.

Everything felt different now.

7

The killer watched, lurking in the safety of the shadows in the corner of the car park. His plan was working. He could tell Sam Cobbs was slipping he could see it. He held the binoculars up again when he saw her standing at her office window, the doubt in her eyes evident as she took in the view of the surrounding hills. She was second-guessing her instincts. It was beautiful to witness. There was nothing finer than watching an SIO sink fast, tightrope-walking on a precipice.

Truth was a significant weapon.

And lies? They were an art.

He would wait until she was home and send her a message, an untraceable text to her mobile. He knew the effect it would have on her fragile state of mind. Did he care? Not one bit. He laughed and slipped away.

SAM MADE a conscious effort to shake the tension out of her body as she entered Doreen's house to pick up Tilly after work. "How has she been today?"

Doreen frowned. Sam got the impression that Doreen sensed there was something wrong.

"Perfect as always. She's a little treasure, sent from Heaven. Now, no beating about the bush, Sam, you look exhausted. Let me make you a drink. I'm not going to take no for an answer."

Sam smiled and sat on the sofa. She played with Tilly until Doreen reappeared with a mug of coffee.

"Now, tell me what's on your mind. Is it the investigation you're working on, love? Is that what's getting you down? If you don't mind me saying, you look as miserable as sin, and yet you have your wedding coming up in a few weeks."

Sam stared at Tilly. The tears emerged and dripped onto her cheek.

"Sam, my dear. Please tell me. Don't keep me in the dark. I'm worried about you."

"I'm sorry, Doreen. I didn't want to burden you with this. It's Rhys."

Doreen's hand covered her chest. "What about him? He hasn't left you, has he? He's usually home long before this. I was wondering where he had got to this evening."

"No. We believe he's been kidnapped. I think the killer we're chasing has abducted him."

Doreen's mouth dropped open, and her hands began to tremble.

Sam knelt beside her and comforted her. "No, no, I shouldn't have told you."

Doreen's lip quivered. "I'm glad you have. How? What are you doing about it? I don't mean that nastily, as if you're not doing anything... I'm sorry, I wasn't criticising you. I can't imagine the torment you must be going through."

"It's okay. It's natural for you to ask. We've had men out there since just after lunch. I met him for a coffee earlier... He disappeared not long after he left me. Bob and I retraced his steps back to the office, but... came up blank."

"Oh, my goodness. No wonder you're down, dear. This is heart-breaking. You know if there's anything I can do, you only have to ask. If you need me to look after Tilly for longer, well, you know the offer is always on the table. One thing is puzzling me. You told me the killer has him. Have they made contact with you to confirm that?"

"No. But experience tells me that this person has him. We've recently found out that Rhys is linked to a place that has been highlighted during our investigation."

Doreen frowned and shook her head. "I don't understand. You don't have to tell me, but it might ease your burden if you confide in me, Sam. You know it won't go any further."

"That goes without saying. I trust you unreservedly. Do you remember a children's home which closed down years ago called Pendle House?"

Doreen's eyes widened. "Yes, of course I do. It was linked to some kind of scandal back in the day, wasn't it? I can't for the life of me remember what that was... Hang on, yes, I can. It was an outrage about the children being abused. Or am I wrong?"

"No, you've got it spot on."

"How was Rhys involved? He didn't..."

Sam hugged Doreen, then sat back down next to Tilly. "No, not as far as I know. I asked him about his experience, and he told me he had only worked there for three weeks. It was part of his university course."

"And he never told you?"

Tears stung. "No. That's what I'm struggling with. I had trouble processing the information. It caused a rift between us last night, and when another body was discovered this morning, I rang him and arranged to meet him at a café. I plucked up the courage to confront him about it, and we both said things we shouldn't have. He ended up walking out on me. I'm totally to blame, and now I'm riddled with guilt because he's gone missing."

"You can't blame yourself, Sam. Please don't do it. It'll eat you alive and prevent you from carrying out your job properly. For your own sake, rid yourself of that guilt this evening."

Sam took a sip from her coffee and nodded. "You're right. I don't know if I'll be able to do that, though. There's more, something I have been keeping from you for a few days."

"And what's that, love? Come on, let it out. You can trust me."

"I've spoken about her before, Claire Owen. Do you remember?"

"The name sounds familiar. Isn't she a member of your team?"

"She is. Or should I say was. She was murdered yesterday."

"No! Don't tell me her death is linked to the investigation?"

"It is. Furthermore, during the day, it's come to our attention that she was also connected to Pendle House. We believe she uncovered something important which ultimately led to her death. We've since found an email from the killer, requesting that she meet them at the harbour on the night she died."

"And she didn't tell you? I'm sensing a pattern here."

Sam sighed. "Yes. God, it has been eating away at me all day, the fact that both Claire and Rhys have deceived me over the years."

Doreen wagged her finger. "You mustn't think that, Sam. There must be a reason they both kept the information from you. I'm not saying it was intentional, but there must be some reason why they didn't tell you."

"I've got a lot of thinking to do this evening. First, I'm going to drink my coffee, and then I'm going to take Tilly for a walk. I'm sure it'll help clear my head."

"I agree. Walking, especially on a lovely evening like tonight, will be good for your mental health."

Sam smiled and finished her coffee. "I'm going to love you and leave you. Thanks for letting me bend your ear. Sorry if you found the revelation about Rhys upsetting."

"It's life, sweetheart. Think about Rhys and the time you've shared together so far. Don't let his past, and the horrors it holds, define your future. I'll keep my fingers crossed that he's returned to us safely."

Sam hugged her friend. "Thank you for being you. You truly brighten my life."

"That's the sweetest thing to say. You know I regard you as family, Sam. I'm always here for you. Please, please remember that."

"I will. I'm forever in your debt, kind lady."

. . .

AFTER HER WALK and feeding Tilly, Sam turned her attention to cobbling together an evening meal for herself from the limited food she found in the fridge. "Looks like omelette for tea this evening, girl. Cheese and tomato, with a few chunks of pepper and bacon thrown into the mix."

As she watched the egg mixture cook, her thoughts wandered back to Rhys and what must be happening to him, if she was right and he had been abducted by the killer. A burning smell brought her back to the here and now. "Shit! I can't even make my own dinner properly. What's the frigging chance of rescuing my bloody fiancé?" She flipped the omelette in the pan and sighed. "Burnt offerings on the menu for this evening, Tilly. Even your dinner seems more appetising than what I'm about to eat."

Her mobile tinkled. A message had arrived. She closed her eyes and uttered a silent prayer that it was from Rhys.

WHEN YOU FIND out the ones closest to you lie, who do you become?

SAM STARED at the message and reread it three times, her stomach twisting and her heart racing. Caller ID not recognised. No signature —as if there would be. Nothing.

He was taunting her, letting her know that he had Rhys. She considered calling Bob but feared what the repercussions would be if she did. The killer was watching her, striking the litmus paper and daring her to crumble.

Again, the same doubts she had experienced during the day resurfaced. Who could she trust?

Did she have it in her to remain focused? A ripple of fear reverberated through her body.

Do I have it in me to counter yet another serial killer who appears intent on coming after me and the people closest to me? I have to warn my family, just in case.

Fortunately, her father and Margaret were overseas in the Channel Islands, so she didn't feel it necessary to worry them. She rang Crystal, her sister, and spilled the truth.

"What? No, you can't be serious. Why do these feckers keep going after Rhys?" Crystal asked.

"Pass. Ask me another. The problem is, I don't know who this bastard is going to come after next. I need you and Vernon to stay somewhere else for a few days. Out of danger. Just until we've caught the fucker."

"Where can we go?"

"I don't know. Rent a cottage. I'll pay if necessary."

"This is insane, Sam. Who would come after you and your family like this?"

Sam explained what she and her team had been tackling since the first murder had landed on her desk and the connection between the victims. "You see what we're up against here? The killer has already taken out one of my team and abducted my fiancé. I wouldn't ask you to leave your home if I didn't feel it was important, sis."

"All right. I'll see what we can come up with between us and let you know what we decide later. Silly question coming up: how are you holding up?"

Sam smiled. "Apart from burning my omelette, fair to middling."

"Sounds delicious. Sending hugs. I love you, Sam, more than life itself. I don't tell you nearly enough."

"Don't, you'll start me off. I love you to the moon and back. I always have."

Sam cleaned up the kitchen and let Tilly in the back garden to have an extra wee before they went up to bed. She planned to watch some TV upstairs before she turned in for the night. She ended up staring at the screen for the next three hours and eventually turned it off around eleven, hoping that sleep would soon come her way. It didn't. Tilly spent a restless night beside her. It was as if she knew something bad had happened to Rhys, which only made Sam more agitated.

In the end, she finally fell asleep at four a.m. Even then, she kept waking up, perspiring, after dreaming about the torture Rhys might be going through. Her alarm buzzed at seven. After a quick shower, she dressed and took Tilly for her morning walk before heading into work.

8

S am arrived at work and summoned the team together. She had no intention of telling them about the message she had received. Bob had dropped by her office as soon as he'd got there to check how she had coped the evening before. He seemed distressed by her appearance, although he tried not to show it.

"Right, as far as I can tell, there have been no developments overnight." *In other words, Rhys's body hasn't been discovered yet, or if it has, we haven't received word of it. Otherwise, Jason would have told me on my way in this morning.* "I want you to finish off going through the list of names we have from the back of the photo. Try to track down the ones you didn't speak to yesterday. I believe this could be important. Maybe the suggestion Bob made about one of them being the killer is true. Who knows? The more people we speak to, the better. Bob, can you get on to the council and ask them to hand over any files they have about Pendle House? I'm guessing they'll request a warrant, but it's worth a try, and yes, you can tell them about the investigation, as nothing has appeared on the news yet."

"Okay, I'll still keep it sketchy and see what I can get out of them."

"We also need to go over the other idea that surfaced late yesterday, before we left for the evening. Liam, I'd like you to thoroughly go through Claire's computer. Specifically, her search history. Let's see what she's been working on, for Lord knows how long, behind our backs. It could turn out to be the key and tell us how the killer found out about her and what she was up to."

Bob's brow furrowed. "You think she might have triggered a file on the computer? A website perhaps?"

Sam shrugged. "Your guess is as good as mine. I'm just throwing it out there, partner. It's not like we've got anything else to go on, is it? I don't have to remind you all of the need for speed and accuracy in obtaining this information. Rhys is still missing. That fact alone should be enough to urge us on. I'm clinging on to the other important fact that is staring us in the face: his body hasn't been found yet. Until it is, there's every chance we might find him alive, safe and well..." Her voice trailed off. That was the hope. She needed to get the urgency across to her team, but inside, she was crying out to be out there, scouring the streets to find him.

She had woken up in a slightly more forgiving mood; however, she had no idea how long that would last. "I'll be in my office, dealing with my usual mundane task." She closed the door behind her. On the way to her seat, she paused to admire the view as usual, but this time, her gaze dropped below her to a figure she thought she saw in the corner of the car park. The sunlight glinted on something. She turned and ran out of the office, took the stairs two at a time and sprinted through the reception area. By the time she reached the spot where she'd seen the person lingering, it was too late.

Seconds later, she received another text:

Close, but not close enough. You're slacking, Inspector Cobbs. One more slip-up and it could signify the end for someone close to you. Do I mean Rhys? Or do I have someone else in mind? Maybe your sister or her husband. Both celebrities in their own right within the town. I'll be in touch soon, Inspector. Until then, happy hunting. Not all roads lead to the truth, don't forget that.

Sam heaved out a sigh and headed back to the station. Bob was standing at the entrance.

"Is everything all right? Did you forget something in the car?"

She was in two minds whether to reveal the truth or not. "I thought I saw someone lurking in the shadows. It was my imagination playing me up."

"Christ, don't do that to me. If it happens again, promise me you'll ask either me or another member of the team to go with you. What if it had turned out to be the killer? You wouldn't have stood a chance; you had no weapon with you. Why take the risk? With what's been going on, it's too dangerous for you to be out there alone. Got that?"

Sam stroked his arm. "Thanks for caring. Message received, partner. You have my word; I won't do it again. Come on, let's get back to work. I'm in need of a caffeine fix. I think I've missed my usual quota for this time of the morning."

"Easily sorted."

They reached the main office. "I'll be in my cave. Can you bring my drink in, Bob?"

He nodded and fixed the drinks, offering to make one for the entire team while he was at it.

He delivered her coffee and said, "Don't tell me, I've missed my vocation in life."

A glimmer of a smile tugged at her lips. "I'm saying nothing. Thanks, Bob, for everything."

"For checking to see if you're all right? Are you sure you're not keeping something from me?"

"You know me better than that. I wouldn't do it."

His eyes formed tiny slits. "That's debatable. I'll leave you to it, for now."

"Give me a shout if you discover anything interesting."

He saluted and closed the door behind him.

Before she started on her post, Sam picked up the phone and rang her sister. "Crystal, it's me."

"I know. It tells me that on my little screen. Marvellous inventions, these new smartphones. They're smarter than some adults I know."

"All right, smart arse... see what I did there? Anyway, I'm just checking in with you to see if you've managed to secure a bolthole for the next few days."

"I have, but I'm not going to tell you. That's the wisest thing, isn't it? What if the killer is monitoring your phones?"

"Oh God, you're on top form. I never even considered that. When do you head off?"

"That's need-to-know information. Again, I don't think you should know."

"I'll call you back on another line." She ended the call, bolted out of her chair and walked towards Bob at speed. He ducked, sensing that she was about to clobber him when she held out her hand.

"What in God's name are you doing, man?"

"Protecting myself."

"You're a damn idiot. All I'm after is your phone."

"What? Why?"

"Just because I can."

"You think the killer is monitoring your calls, is that it?"

"It's a precaution I'm willing to take."

He handed his phone over, and she returned to her office to call her sister back. "It's me again. I'm using Bob's phone."

"You're presuming that one is safe?"

"I have to. Give me the address of where you'll be staying, just in case."

"God... you're now scaring the shit out of me, Sam."

"Sorry, that's not my intention, I promise. All I'm trying to do is keep you safe."

"What about Dad? Have you contacted him?"

"No. I reckon he should be safe, being overseas at the moment. Address?" she prompted a second time.

"As it happens, after we spoke last night, Vernon rang around a few of his mates. One of them is away for the week. He's told us we can stay there, provided we don't have any wild parties."

"As if that's likely to happen at your age. Oops, sorry, that slipped out."

"You wait until I see you. You'll pay for that."

"I still need the address, Crystal."

Sam jotted it down. "I'll arrange for a drive-by now and again, if only to ease my mind."

"Thanks, I think. I appreciate your willingness to keep us safe; however, it's a little disconcerting that you're having to do it in the first place."

"I'm doing it because I love you."

"Before you go, I don't suppose there's been any news on Rhys overnight, has there?"

"Nothing at all, which is why I'm doing my best to ensure you stay safe. I'm glad you're not fighting me on this one, sis. Thank you for trusting me."

"I'd trust you with my life. I'll keep in touch. Maybe you should invest in a new phone."

"I've got an old phone in my drawer. I'll see if I can revive that and get it working. Take care and remain vigilant, Crystal."

"I will. Don't worry about us. Promise me you'll do the same. Think before you make a decision, and never go anywhere on your own. Take Bob with you."

"I will. Don't worry. Love you."

"Love you more."

Sam ended the call and returned the phone to Bob. "Thanks. I wanted to call Crystal. I've told her and Vernon to go away for a few days, you know, to keep them out of harm's way. I'll get back to it."

"Great idea. We can't be too careful... after Rhys going missing. But I don't have to tell you that. It sounds to me like you have it all in hand."

Sam winked at him and returned to the office.

THE POST TOOK LONGER than normal for her to complete. She was amazed that she didn't find herself distracted throughout the mundane task, which left her wondering if she had truly forgiven Rhys or not. She joined the rest of the team. Liam was at the drinks station, making everyone another cup of coffee.

"How's it going? And please don't tell me slowly," Sam asked. She perched on the edge of the desk adjacent to Bob's.

"As it happens, I was about to come and see you to bring you up to date on what we've found."

Sam leaned in and rested her hands on her thighs. "I'm all ears."

"Liam has been busy going through Claire's files, and he discovered one that sparked his interest. Claire had decrypted the file. It showed the same list of people who were in that photo, but there was someone who wasn't."

"I'm intrigued. Go on."

Liam handed Sam and Bob a coffee each and went to collect the others. "Well done, Liam. Not just for making the coffee but for finding the file."

"It was nothing really, boss. I tried to think outside the box and opened file after file until I found it buried inside another one. It's the type of thing I used to do when I was growing up because I didn't want my brother reading my personal stuff. Times were hard, and we were forced to share a computer."

"Worth knowing. Thanks for the tip. Sorry, Bob, you were saying?"

"Ivy Renshaw. I've checked the employee records. She used to be the housemaid at Pendle. She left suddenly back in 2006. No forwarding address. No exit interview on file. Nothing. She just vanished."

"Can you bring up the file?"

"I can. I did some extra digging and found a photo of the woman on her personnel file." He enlarged the photo on the screen.

Sam stared at it. There was something familiar about her, but she couldn't for the life of her figure out what it was.

"Are you all right? Do you know her?"

"I'm not sure. I think I recognise her face. And she definitely wasn't in the other photo we have?"

"No, she's not on there. I double-checked before I mentioned it."

Sam scratched her head as a smidgen of an idea came to her. She shoved Bob out of the way and pounded his keyboard, searching for something in particular. She brought up a different image and compared the two. "Isn't that her?"

"What is this?"

"Rhys has the same photo at home, sitting in his office. It was taken at a recent charity event he organised at the university he attended. I think it might have been to raise funds for a different children's home."

The woman was there in the photo, older, worn down but unmistakable nonetheless. She appeared to be in the background, all alone, watching.

"She hasn't vanished at all. Let's see if we can find out whether she's using the same name. Bob, can you get a list of attendees for the charity event for me?"

"I'll do my best. It seems to be busy there. We could be looking at thousands."

"Needs must. We have to find out who she is and what name she's using these days. She appears to be alone. Let's work on that, for now."

TWO HOURS LATER, with everyone lending a hand, they found the woman in the photo was Michele Turner. Liam did some extra digging and discovered yet another link to Rhys in the woman's background.

"I've got her working at a private care home on the outskirts of Workington. I found another couple of photos, and I'm sorry to have to tell you, boss, that Turner and Rhys were at the same facility. It's possible that he either worked or volunteered there during his summer break from uni."

"Crap, and he's not around to either confirm or deny knowing her," Sam said.

"There would be no point, not if we have the proof," Bob pointed out.

. . .

THE REST of the day was spent trying to find Michele Turner. She wasn't entered on the electoral register. This led Sam to believe that she could now be living under yet another assumed name. Sam dismissed the team at six that evening. Everyone was down, feeling the frustration of the investigation. She had decided against asking a member of the team to remain on duty to cover another few hours. What was the point? Apart from seeing the person who she presumed was the killer in the car park, she'd had no further contact with them. Had the figure looked like a woman? She wasn't sure about that either.

Sam drove home. She parked outside her property as a message came through.

YOU'RE LOOKING in the wrong direction, Inspector Cobbs. The truth doesn't always wear a mask, or maybe it does!

WHAT THE FUCK is that supposed to mean? Does it, or doesn't it? Is the killer purposely trying to confuse me?

She didn't react openly to the message because she spotted Doreen watching her from the lounge window. Sam smiled, and her neighbour opened the door to let her in. Tilly was there, jumping up and wanting a cuddle.

"Get down, monkey. You know you're not supposed to jump up."

"Aww... she's missed you. She's been crying today, Sam. I tried to hug her, to comfort her, but she wouldn't have it."

"I'm sorry if she's been a nuisance. I'll take her for a longer walk than usual and pick up a takeaway on the way back; it'll save me from burning another dinner tonight."

"Don't spend out. I can knock you up an omelette; it's no trouble."

Sam smiled. "I had that as burnt offerings last night. It was so bad, I think it's turned me off them for life, but thanks for the offer. Do you fancy fish and chips, or have you already eaten?"

"I have, although that does sound tempting. Maybe I'll have a small portion. Will they do that for me?"

"I'm sure they get asked all the time. I'll see what I can do. It'll be another hour or so."

"Let me get you some money."

Sam raised her hand. "No, this is on me, to make up for this little one being a pain in the backside."

"It's not necessary. I take it there's no news about Rhys?"

"Nothing. It's so disappointing. I'm clinging on to the fact that his body hasn't shown up yet."

"I don't blame you. It's a definite positive."

Sam fastened Tilly's harness and headed towards the park. They circled the park for nearly an hour. It did Sam the world of good, and Tilly seemed happy enough with her longer walk as well. She stopped off at the chippy and placed the order from the doorway rather than take Tilly inside. The girl serving came to collect the money from her.

She rushed home and ate her dinner with Doreen. It was good for both of them to have some company at that time of the day. They chatted about this, that and the other for the next two hours until Sam started yawning.

"I'm sorry, I'd better go home now. It's been lovely spending time with you, Doreen."

"It has, sweetheart. Sleep well, Sam. I'm always here, remember that. I'll see you in the morning when you drop the little one off. Come here, Tilly." The pup walked sideways towards Doreen and allowed her to pet her head. "Oh my, what's happening with Casper? I should have asked this morning, but I wasn't fully awake when you dropped her off."

"I rang Brenda earlier. She loves taking care of Casper and has agreed to keep him with her until the situation with Rhys is resolved."

"Let's hope that's soon, Sam. Maybe that's why Tilly was unsettled today, because she misses Casper as well as Rhys."

Sam nodded. "You could be right. I never gave it a second thought. I'll give her a belly full of treats before we go to bed."

THE FOLLOWING MORNING, the weather was dreary and miserable, just like her mood. She drove into work, her thoughts heavy with Renshaw and the growing web of deceit surrounding this investigation.

Bob was waiting for her in the reception area.

She shook off the rain and asked, "What's up?"

"This was left for us at the front desk by a youngster. He told the desk sergeant that someone wearing a hood asked him to drop it off."

He held out a photo in his gloved hand. It was of the station car park. More importantly, it was focused on both Sam's and Bob's vehicles, taken from a distance. Scrawled across the bottom in smudged ink were the words, **You brought the past into your present. Now watch it bleed.**

Bob glanced at Sam as if he knew the answer to what the message meant. It was time to reveal the truth. "Let's go upstairs. I have something I need to tell you."

He huffed and puffed his way up the flight of concrete steps to the main office and threw himself into his chair. Crossing his arms, he demanded, "Let's have it. I had a feeling you've been keeping me in the dark about something."

"I haven't... not intentionally. It's only been a day or so since the first message arrived."

"What message? Or should I say messages? Sam, we're a bloody team. I should have been told. I know you're suffering from trust issues at the moment, I get that, but bloody hell..."

"I was in the wrong. I'm sorry. You have every right to be mad at me." She handed him the phone, and he read the messages she had received.

"Jesus, this is serious. Wait a minute... yesterday, when you rushed outside... why? What did you see?"

"I believe the killer was out there, watching me. I caught a glimpse of someone and decided to run downstairs to challenge the person, but they legged it before I could get there."

"But you denied it, said it was your imagination when I suggested... Why didn't you tell me? You do realise how dangerous that could have been?"

"I do now. It won't happen again. You know what all of this means, don't you?"

"Let me guess... that we're closing in on him or her. For all we know, this Renshaw woman might be the killer."

She nodded, a lump forming in her throat that she struggled to shift. Rather than break down in front of her partner, she made them both a coffee. While she was doing this, the rest of the team arrived. Bob took the pressure off her and filled the team in himself about the messages Sam had received.

"We need to trace the phone they came from," Nick suggested. "I can do that, or should I say, I know a man who can do it for us."

Sam gave him the thumbs-up. "Get on it ASAP, Nick."

Nick's friend came up trumps within an hour. The message was traced to a phone which was on and located at a derelict warehouse near the harbour in Whitehaven. Sam and Bob drove to the location. They found signs of someone having recently been there, but they were already gone. They were about to leave when Sam spotted something poking out from one of the crates.

"What's this?" She removed a pair of gloves from her pocket and slipped them on. "It's a folder."

Sam opened it, and inside she found newspaper articles about Pendle House. Each of them had circles around a specific name: Claire Owen, Weller, Trigg, Rhys. And now... she rubbed at her eyes, not believing what she was reading. One more name she had not been expecting: Bob Jones. There was a final page that had one word written on it:

DECIDE.

. . .

Bob stared at her. "What does that mean?"

Sam's mind was spinning. "It means we've run out of time."

The killer was closing in.

They drove back to the station in silence.

Bob followed her from the car through the reception area and into her office at her request. He closed the door as she lowered the blind.

They both took a seat.

Sam glared at him, not knowing how to begin the conversation. "Just when I thought it couldn't get any worse. Why is your name in that file, Bob? The truth. Don't give me any bullshit. I deserve to be told the truth, so tell me."

Bob rubbed his hands together, his gaze fixed on the wall behind her. "It's not what it seems."

"Isn't it? I'll be the judge of that."

"Sam, you've got to trust me. Doesn't all our years working together as partners mean anything to you?"

"Don't pull that one. How can I trust you? You're just the same as Claire and Rhys, keeping your nasty little secrets close to your chest. People are dying all around us, and here you are, telling me it's not what it seems."

He sighed and shook his head over and over. "It's not, I swear. I was newly qualified, fresh out of training school. I was assigned to an incident at Pendle House, just the one report. A girl went missing for two days and then turned up injured. They tried to tell us it was a mistake, the girl had run away after an argument with another girl. My sergeant signed it off."

"And you let it go?"

"What else was I supposed to do? I did raise the question, but the sergeant slapped me down, told me to move on and forget about it. He warned me that if I didn't let it go, it could ruin my career. So I buried it, Sam."

Flummoxed, she stared at him for a long time, betrayal twisting a knife in her chest. "All this time..."

"Let's be fair about this. It's not like I've lied to you on purpose, is it? All this happened a long time ago. The same for Rhys. Treating him the way you did... well, that's worked out well, hasn't it?"

Sam sat there and shook her head. "Don't you dare put this back on me. Can you imagine what I'm going through right now, knowing that the people closest to me have been living with secrets all these years?"

"I refuse to be held accountable for something I did nearly twenty years ago. I haven't lied to you or betrayed you. If anything, it was an incident that I had forgotten about, until recently."

"Until people started dying because of their connection to Pendle House. That was the time to tell me, to reveal you had a connection to that place, no matter how small or insignificant you thought it might have been. But nothing. Zilch. You've carried on as if..." She choked up, and her eyes pricked with threatening tears, not for the first time over the past couple of days. *Why am I getting so upset about people lying and keeping stuff from me...? Hang on, am I not doing the same thing, keeping my boss out of the loop?* She was getting sick to death of dealing with her emotions at work and was desperate to find an off switch.

He looked at her, shame written in every line of his face. "I never wanted to lie to you..."

"But you did. My dilemma is, and it's a huge one, I just don't know who I can trust any more. I've never felt this way before... and I don't mind admitting that it's suffocating the fucking life out of me."

Not knowing what else to say, Bob shrugged and left the office.

Am I losing my touch as a copper? Why hadn't I noticed that I was being lied to by everyone around me? As soon as Pendle House came to our attention, everyone I knew should have told me what they knew about that place... Instead, they kept it hidden. How am I supposed to deal with that? Set it aside and ignore the deceit? How is that going to help?

Unlike her, Sam chose to spend the rest of the day in her office away from the others, needing the time to reflect and to consider whether she still had it in her to make the right decisions needed to rescue Rhys. She put the blind up and stared out of the window, scouring the car park for anyone lurking in the shadows beneath the trees at the rear. Today, the area appeared to be clear. She questioned whether she would have the ability to tackle anyone in the future, given the way she was feeling. It was as if all her enthusiasm for the job had diminished overnight, and no matter how hard she searched, she couldn't find the right emotions to put it right.

She sent the team home at six. Bob remained behind; he appeared to be full of remorse.

She brushed past him. "I can't deal with this right now. I'll see you tomorrow. I have a lot to consider this evening."

"Like what? Sam, please... it was a mistake. I should have told you, confided in you long ago. I realise that now. Please, give me another chance to prove myself worthy of being your partner."

"That's something I need to think about. We all know what happens once someone's trust in you is broken."

"Are you talking about terminating our partnership? You can't be serious... not over something so..."

"So what? Minor?" she finished for him. "It might have been minor in your eyes, but trust and loyalty mean everything to me. That's the end of this conversation. I'm leaving now. Switch off the lights on your way out." Sam grabbed her bag and coat and flew past him without saying another word.

She drove home on autopilot, her adrenaline pumping. No sooner had she left the station than she drew up outside her cottage, or so it had seemed. She knocked on Doreen's door to collect Tilly.

"Sam, are you all right?" Doreen asked.

"I think so. I've had a pig of a day, and I'm in dire need of a walk with this little one. Sorry, Doreen, I'm going to grab her and run this evening, if that's okay?"

"You do as you see fit, love. Just answer me one thing before you go."

"What's that?"

"Any news about Rhys?"

Sam sighed. "Not a dicky bird. It's been a trying day for all of us. In all honesty, I'm not sure how much more I can take... sorry, I shouldn't have said that. Goodnight, see you soon."

"I'm getting the sense that you need to talk, but I don't want to push you, Sam."

"Thanks, Doreen. I'd be a blubbering mess if I stopped to chat now. I can't seem to control my emotions today."

"It's only natural, given the circumstances."

Sam hugged her neighbour, popped Tilly's harness on, then set off for the park. She wished there was somewhere else she could go within walking distance. The park brought back too many memories of how she and Rhys met while she was still married to Chris—and look how that had ended. As she walked, she contemplated the amount of shit that had been sent her way over the last few years. She dared anyone not to feel the way she did at that moment. Add the betrayal of her work colleagues, not to mention Rhys's, and bang... how the fuck was she supposed to react?

Tilly tried to pull her towards the tree a squirrel had just scampered up. "Not so fast, sweetie. Let's just have a leisurely walk at Mummy's pace for a change. I need to learn to chill, to take my foot off the accelerator now and again. Maybe that will be beneficial to me."

Tilly whimpered, desperate to get to another squirrel that ran past them barely five feet away.

"Come on you. Let's go home." The walk had satisfied Tilly's needs, and she appeared to be a lot calmer now. Sam withdrew her phone from her jacket pocket and made a call. "Pick up, you ignorant so-and-so."

The phone rang out until Bob's voicemail kicked in. "You've reached Bob Jones. You've got this far; you might as well leave a message. I'll get back to you soon."

She glanced down at Tilly casually trotting beside her, her tail wagging. "I think he's ignoring me, and who could blame him after what I said to him today? I'll leave him to stew this evening and make it up to him in the morning."

Sam waved at Doreen, who was in her usual spot, keeping an eye out for when they got back. They exchanged a thumbs-up, and Sam opened the front door. Tilly ran ahead of her. The day had been a damp one, and it had negatively impacted the temperature inside the house. She switched on the heating for just half an hour to take the chill off.

After feeding Tilly, she searched the freezer for one of Rhys's batch meals he had recently knocked up. She kicked herself for not having the time to stop off at the supermarket and stock up the fridge. Eventually, she found a meatball dish with rice and put it in the microwave to defrost. While she waited, she rang Bob's number again. She kicked out at the stool as the answerphone spewed out its inane message.

Furious that Bob was choosing to ignore her, she poured herself a glass of red wine to go with her meal. Tilly sat beside her, waiting for scraps. Sam left her some rice and sauce, making sure there was no onion in her bowl before she gave it to her. She rinsed her plate under the running tap, switched off the heating now the house felt warmer and put the TV on in the lounge. The local news was running the story about the murders that she and her team had been investigating all week. It highlighted her need to speak to Bob and apologise for the way she had treated him. Her walk had given her time to think and reflect, and she had realised she was in the wrong for taking it out on him. She was eager to put things right, and the only way she could do that was in person.

"Come on, girl. Let's go for a ride."

She put Tilly in the back seat and waved at Doreen. Her old neighbour looked worried at seeing her drive off again so soon after getting home. Tilly curled up in a ball, sensing something wasn't right.

"Hey, it's going to be okay, sweetheart. I promise. Bob and I have fallen out before over the years. He's just winding me up. Playing hard to get, that's all. Everything will be fine, trust me."

There was that word again... trust!

She arrived at Bob's address and hit out at the steering wheel. His car was parked on the drive. *I was right; he is home. Bloody ignorant sod.* There were no lights on inside the house. Sam left her vehicle, and as she walked across the road, she could see the front door was ajar. She

The Truth Will Out

recalled Bob had told her that Abigail and their daughter were away, visiting Abigail's parents. She crept closer, eyes and ears alert. The hallway was empty; their house was colder than hers. She shivered, regretting not wearing a jacket.

Inside, the lounge was in chaos: drawers pulled out of the sideboard, cushions from the sofa scattered across the floor, and on the coffee table, she found a message written in blood.

YOU BURIED THE TRUTH. **I'm digging it back up.**

SAM'S PULSE roared in her ears. She spun in place, her heart hammering, not knowing what to do next.

Where the hell is he? Stop it! Get a grip and do something to help Bob!

Out of the corner of her eye, she spotted Bob's phone. She crossed the room to check it. The screen was cracked.

He couldn't have answered it, even if it had rung. Where is he?

She fished her own phone out, made the call to the station, then searched the rest of the house. Bob was gone. It was silly to believe his disappearance wasn't connected to the investigation.

It seemed like an eternity before a patrol arrived. She handed the scene over to them then rushed home to drop Tilly off at Doreen's. En route, she rang the other three members of her team, requesting that they join her back at the station.

The first thing she did when she arrived was to put out an alert across Cumbria. She left that in the desk sergeant's capable hands and flew up the stairs. The rest of the team arrived not long after. Everyone was shocked when she explained what had happened.

"It's obvious the killer has him. I found a message written in blood at Bob's house. I get the impression the perpetrator is watching my every move."

"What did the message say, boss?" Liam was the first to ask.

"'You buried the truth. I'm digging it back up.' I don't mind admitting that I'm scared. Worried about what this crazy fucker is going to do next."

Between them, they spent the next hour or so bouncing ideas around until another message arrived—this time from a different number. She read the message out: "'You didn't listen. Now someone else must pay.'" Attached was a photo of Bob, unconscious and slumped in a chair, his wrists tied to the arms, a dark stain covering his white shirt.

"Shit! I can't do this," Sam said. She perched on the desk behind her, eyes wide open, and stared at the wall in front of her.

"Boss, you can't give up now, not when they both need us," Oliver said.

Nick approached Sam and, having known her the longest, took charge of the situation. He gripped her shoulders and gave them a slight shake. "Sam, you've got this. We've got this. You're not alone. We're all here to support you. We dropped everything to be here and help you through this. Don't give up now. You've led us through worse, Sam."

Sam tipped her head back and inhaled a few deep breaths. Nick took a step back.

She shook out her arms and nodded. "Thanks for your support, guys. With you all beside me, hopefully, we'll find Bob and Rhys and bring down this evil individual." She refused to call this person a killer, not while they still had Rhys, and now Bob.

Another message arrived.

YOU HAVE ONE HOUR. **Come alone. Or he dies.**

"WHAT THE FUCK? Where? He hasn't given me an address. Does he mean for me to return to the warehouse?"

"I don't think so," Oliver said. "Why use a different phone? We need to trace the number and get the coordinates."

"In an hour? How are we supposed to do that?" Sam said, mortified.

"Leave it with me," Nick said. He rang his friend again. "Cheers, as quick as you can. It's a matter of life or death, mate." He ended the call. "Adam reckons he can have the results back to us within thirty minutes."

"I think we should get on the road," Oliver suggested.

"But the message says to come alone. If he or she is watching me, they'll know you guys are with me."

"We take two cars," Liam suggested. "We let you go first and set off behind you after a few minutes. We can stay in contact via the radio on a frequency used only by us."

"That's a great idea," Nick and Oliver said in unison.

Another message tinkled. Sam grabbed her phone and gasped. "It's from Rhys's number."

WATCH AND LEARN, **Inspector.**

HER BLOOD TURNED COLD. Two people she cared about, both abducted and in the hands of this crazy person. Who could she turn to for help? She had the rest of the team beside her, but were they going to be enough?

AS PLANNED, they left the station. Nick's mate, Adam, had come through at the last minute and given them the coordinates of a warehouse close to the edge of Workington. It was abandoned, forgotten about and ripe for development.

She pulled up outside what appeared to be the entrance. Alone, as instructed. The rest of the team were close by. If they didn't hear from her within fifteen minutes, they had her permission to come looking for her. Sam removed her Taser from the passenger seat and tucked it into the rear of her trousers, ensuring her jacket hid it.

Dusk had already descended. She removed her phone from her pocket, having had the foresight to put it on charge during the journey, and turned on the torch.

"Hello," she called out.

Her footsteps echoed, and a mixture of distasteful, unrecognisable smells hit her nostrils. Receiving no reply, she wandered through the debris to what appeared to be a room at the back. Heart pounding, she turned the handle and eased the door open. She saw the outline of a figure sitting in a chair. She shone the torch at the person.

"Bob. My God! Are you all right?"

He was barely conscious, although he managed a groan when he saw her. He was tied to the same chair as in the photo, blood oozing from a wound on his shoulder. A camera was set up on a tripod facing him. She ran a hand around his face.

"Bob, I'm sorry. I'm here to rescue you. Stay with me. Please, stay with me!"

He moaned and licked his dry lips. "We got this all wrong... It's not about... revenge... it's about *cleansing*."

Sam stiffened. "What? Do you know who is behind this? Have they shown themselves to you?"

"No. They were wearing a mask; they knocked me out."

Sam held the torch over his hands. "I need something to help me untie you. Have you seen Rhys? Did they mention him? Is he still alive, Bob?"

Bob's head lolled to the side. "No..." was the only word he whispered before he passed out again.

Sam returned to the doorway, stood still and listened. She strained an ear and heard a whimper. It wasn't close. She had to find the source of the noise, and quickly. There it was again.

She inched forward, stepping over the remains of either a desk or a crate, and headed towards what appeared to be another office. She paused and placed her ear against the door, fearing it might be a trap. Not sensing any immediate danger, she entered the room and gasped. A screen flickered in the corner, and Rhys's face appeared. It was live footage. He was also tied to a chair, just like Bob, not there but somewhere else. Behind him was... Ivy Renshaw, or Michele Turner as she was called now, thanks to a fake ID. Older. Gaunt. Eyes filled with quiet rage.

"I warned you, Inspector Cobbs," the woman's voice echoed through the speaker. "Some truths come with blood. A price tag like no other. You've opened the door... now you need to walk through it."

The screen went black, throwing the room into darkness once more.

Why is she always talking in riddles? What door? The door I've just stepped through?

Time was running out. The rest of the team would be sending out the search party soon. She rang Liam. "I'll make this brief. I've got Bob. Call for an ambulance."

"On it now, boss. Shall we come and help?"

"Yes. Bring something sharp to cut through the thick ropes."

Sam ran back to the room where Bob was being held and waited for the team to arrive. She didn't attempt to remove the ropes in case she ended up tightening them. She spent the time touching her partner's face, feeling guilty about the way she had treated him.

"I'm sorry. I was in the wrong, not you. Don't leave us, Bob. I love you... like a brother," she added swiftly, in case he thought she was confessing her undying love for him.

He stirred and offered her a weak smile. "I didn't mean to... deceive you. Forgive... me... Sam."

"I do. Stay with me; an ambulance is on its way."

"I'm not going anywhere," he whispered. A glimmer of a smile tugged at his dry lips.

"Good. Glad we got that sorted."

THE PARAMEDICS ARRIVED at the location within ten minutes. Bob insisted on walking unaided to the ambulance, but Sam brushed his protests away. His ability to walk was slow and unsteady, but his stubbornness prevailed. In the end, he managed to reach the stretcher under his own steam. The paramedics checked his vital signs.

"We're going to take him in. A doctor needs to see him as soon as possible," the male paramedic said.

Bob opened his mouth to object, but Sam placed a finger on his lips. "Do as they say. It's for the best."

He removed her hand gently. "I'm not leaving you to face this alone," he said, his voice shaky.

"You're forgetting who's in charge. Let the medics do their job, Bob. And for your information, I'm not alone. The rest of the team are right here beside me."

As the paramedics closed the door, Sam turned to Nick and said, "Our priority is to trace where that live feed is coming from. Can you get Adam out here? Will he come?"

"If I ask him to. He owes me. I saved his life when we were on the beat together, back in the day."

"Great stuff. Give him a call."

Nick stepped away from the group and made the call. He returned seconds later, a smile in place. "He's on his way."

"Thanks, Nick. I truly appreciate you calling in a favour for me. We'll need to start with the transmission frequency. I suggest your friend works backwards from the timestamp. I'm going inside to have another look around."

She returned to the warehouse and scanned the room from which she had viewed the live feed. The camera was old, but the broadcasting equipment it was attached to was modern—too modern, Sam suspected, for someone like Michele Turner to have installed the setup herself.

"Someone's helping her," she murmured. She knelt beside the transmitter and examined the small blinking light still active on its side.

A trace signal.

The frustrating part was that now she'd have to wait for Adam to arrive before they could do anything else.

dam unpacked the equipment he needed in the room where Sam had witnessed the live feed. He got down to business straight away.

Sam paced outside the warehouse door, just within earshot.

"Okay, I've got something," he shouted.

Sam and the rest of the team entered the room.

"What have you found?" Sam asked eagerly.

"You did well to spot the trace signal. I worked on that angle first, and here's what I've come up with. It's bouncing through multiple proxies. However, the initial source came from three miles away.

"Lordy, really?" Sam's heart thundered hard enough for it to affect her breathing. She felt the need to change position, leaning against the wall until her breathing rate became stable once more.

Liam, Oliver, and especially Nick, all looked at her, concern etched into their faces.

"Are you all right, boss?" Nick said.

"I will be, in a moment. It's been a hell of a day so far. I can sense we're getting closer now. Sorry, Adam, what I should have asked you is, where? Can you give us the exact location? If not, we're back to square one again. Up the proverbial creek."

He didn't say a word, not until he'd confirmed the coordinates again. "I believe it's somewhere on the northeast side of town, out near the old brickworks. That might even be the location. Do you know that area at all?"

"I'm not that familiar with it. What about you, guys?" she asked her colleagues.

Oliver nodded. "I am. My parents live near there, so I'm a frequent visitor to the area."

"Well, you'll be pleased to know that there's a strong signal still active coming from there. My advice would be to act quickly. If you delay it, there's a chance they might pack up and leave."

"If they do that, we're screwed." Sam inhaled a breath. "Are you guys up for it?"

Each of her colleagues gave a sharp nod.

"Did you all pick up Tasers before we left the station?"

"Absolutely, boss. We're all armed and ready for action," Liam confirmed.

Sam patted Adam on the shoulder. "I hate to do this, but can you come with us, just in case they make a move before we get there? You can bring your equipment and ride with me."

"Wow, that would be amazing. I'd love that... er, from a purely professional point of view, ma'am. In fact, it would be one of my greatest honours."

Nick laughed and tutted. "All right, Adam, there's no need to go over the top about it."

They all laughed as Adam's face flushed. "Sorry. My enthusiasm is probably too much for you peeps. My boss spends most of his time trying to rein me in, not that it does him any good."

Sam grinned. "Less chatter. We'll help you ferry the equipment to the car."

The team lent a hand and, before they jumped back into their vehicles, Sam asked them to gather around.

"I might not have time to say this at the other end, so listen up. We go in quietly. No sirens en route. No radio chatter, in case they're listening in. We do this on our own, with no further backup. Agreed?"

"Agreed, boss," her three colleagues shouted.

"If Michele is there." Sam removed her Taser from its hiding place. She stared at the weapon, wishing it were a gun, and added, "This ends tonight."

IN THE LIGHT of the full moon, the brickworks loomed ahead of them like a relic from the town's darkest days. Sam indicated and drew her car to a halt fifty feet away from the building. She killed her headlights. Oliver did the same in the car behind.

The team gathered closely. "We go in on foot from here in the hope that the element of surprise works in our favour."

Sam led the way. The night had grown chillier. She shuddered and pulled her jacket tighter and did up one of the buttons. She tapped her Taser, hidden in its usual place. It was a relief and a comfort knowing that she was going in there armed and with her colleagues behind her. Ignoring the front entrance, its door left open and inviting them in, Sam discovered an opening at the side of the building. She chose that way in instead, sensing there was every chance the main door might be booby-trapped or at least fitted with a motion sensor that could give them away.

Inside, the internal walls had crumbled in places. Sam studied the ceilings above; she deemed them safe enough for them to continue their journey into the unknown. Her nose twitched; the smell of burning caught her unaware.

Does this mean we're too late? Don't tell me they've tortured him, set him alight and left him to die. There's no sign of life in here so far. No vehicles outside. Am I leading us into a trap? The killer or killers could wipe out the whole team in one go. Shit! Is that their intention?

"Boss, are you all right?" Oliver asked from behind.

"I'm fine. It's too quiet. I hope we're not walking into a trap. Can anyone smell burning?"

"You can't be off it," Liam replied. "We've got your back, boss."

Sam smiled. "What would I do without you guys?" She cocked an ear. "Can you all hear that?"

Oliver strained his neck and said, "Sounds like the hum of a generator."

"I agree. We're going in. I don't have to tell you to keep your wits about you, men. Don't let me down. Keep alert at all times," she whispered her instructions.

Sam followed the sound to a stairwell and glanced up. Her dilemma now was whether she trusted the stairs to take their weight. It would be better if they ascended separately. She gestured silently to make her point. The team all nodded their understanding. Sam withdrew her weapon and cautiously climbed the stairs first. Alert and acutely aware of her surroundings, she waited at the top for the others to join her. In the distance, she could see a heavy metal door. She assumed that was where the generator was housed.

Sam held a finger to her lips. "Stay here. I'm going in alone. I don't want them to know you're here with me. Yes, they might already know if there are cameras downstairs. I'm taking a risk there aren't any. They told me to go to the warehouse alone. They won't be expecting me or us to show up here. Let's use that to our advantage. Stick close; the first sign of trouble, make your move, not until then. Is that understood? If I get into a conversation with anyone, I'll talk louder than usual, hoping that my voice carries."

"Good idea, boss. We'll be right behind you."

Sam raised her thumb and then led the way along the narrow corridor. She pushed open the door that had been left ajar. She was right; there was a generator inside, but that wasn't all. The room was lit by flickering monitors. She got closer. The image was of Rhys. He was bound to a chair, eyes wide and alert, with a figure standing beside him: Michele Turner. She was older. Thinner. Her hair streaked with grey. Her expression was disturbingly calm. Sam went back to the door and called the others in.

"What do you think? Could that room be somewhere in this building?"

"I think it's likely," Oliver said. "There's a lot of open brickwork behind Rhys."

"I was about to say the same," Liam added.

"Where? Downstairs, or could he be on this level?"

"There's a window behind Turner," Nick said. "Can anyone see outside or is it too dark?"

"Too dark," Oliver said. "I'd take a punt on it being downstairs. We could always split up," he suggested.

"No. Not on my watch. Let's stick together."

They made their way back down the staircase one by one and searched the rest of the property, one room at a time, with Sam leading the way as usual. The building was in dire need of either refurbishment or even demolition. Sam followed her instincts and aimed for the rear of the property, assuming it would give the killer an access point.

Another metal door lay ahead of her. She tried the handle; the door was unlocked. She turned to address the team, held her finger to her lips once more, then she pushed open the door. Bingo! She gasped and whispered his name, "Rhys. Are you all right?" As far as she could tell, he was alone. Sam sprinted across the room and dropped to her knees beside him. "My God, what have they done to you?"

"Sam, be careful," he warned. His gaze drifted to the right.

Turner stepped out of the shadows and laughed. "Well, this is a surprise, Inspector. I guess we underestimated your resilience and capabilities."

"Who's *we*? Let him go. Why are you doing this to him?"

"All will be revealed in good time. Stand up," Turner ordered.

Sam hesitantly did as she was instructed. She glanced around her, sensing there was someone else in the room with them, possibly hidden in the shadows. She rested one hand on Rhys's shoulder, assuring him to trust her.

Suddenly, when she least expected it, another person emerged. A man.

Sam gasped a second time. "What the... you? Why?"

Detective Gareth Penn, the lead investigator on the Pendle House sex scandal. He was now retired from the Force. He'd been highly decorated throughout his career and well respected by his colleagues and superiors. How had it come to this—him kidnapping people and killing those involved in the investigation? Anger welled up inside.

He moved to stand next to Michele, syringe in hand, his smile pure evil. "They silenced us, Inspector Cobbs. Covered it up. Brushed the truth under years and years of red tape. But we remember. We remember every scream those children let out. Every secret buried."

Michele swallowed and nodded. "They think justice comes from the reports that were filed. We couldn't stand it any longer. Our aim was to bring truth with pain. It's the only thing these people know: inflicting pain on others."

"Not me. I did nothing wrong," Rhys said, prepared to fight his corner despite his vulnerability. "I was young. I was there only because of my placement. If I had known sooner what was going on under that roof, I would have revealed the truth. I would have told someone in authority. You know me well enough to know that's the truth, Ivy."

"Do I? Yes, our paths have crossed over the years, but do I *really* know you? You had your chance to speak out once you'd left university. You chose to keep your mouth shut, knowing that several children had died at Pendle. I tried my best to protect them... I failed. There was no way I could shield all of them."

On closer inspection, Sam could see that her eyes seemed hollow. They were almost lifeless, as if life had taken its toll on her over the years.

"You did your best," Sam replied. "No one could ask for more. Is that why you left?"

"Yes. I tried to help the children. The owners said I was a fool and ordered me to stop getting in the way. I felt like I was fighting a losing battle. In the end, I threw in the towel. I disappeared. I needed to get my life back on track first. I questioned everything, life itself at times. The horrors of what those children went through haunted me day and night. There were nights I barely slept. We had to do the right thing for the children in the end: avenge their deaths and the torture some of those innocent souls had to endure."

Choosing Ivy's moment of weakness, Sam withdrew her Taser. "Drop the syringe, Penn. Now. This ends here. Rhys did nothing wrong."

Penn took a step forward. "Don't you understand? We had no choice. The people we sought out and killed made it through the cracks. Every one of them wore their guilt like a mask. We took pleasure in stripping that from them."

The door burst open, and the rest of the team barged into the room, Tasers drawn. Penn lunged at Rhys, syringe held high, ready to sink it into his neck. Liam was the first to react. He fired. The Taser wires entered Penn's chest, and he dropped to the floor, fifty thousand volts surging through him.

Michele paused for a moment, then made her move. She searched for the syringe that had landed close to her feet. Sam pounced on her, preferring to tackle the woman herself rather than resort to using her Taser.

"Don't be foolish," Sam snapped, kicking the syringe out of Michele's grasp.

"I need to do it. To get revenge for the children who suffered at the hands of their aggressors."

"You're not listening. Rhys had nothing to do with it."

"He was there. I know he heard the screams. Why won't he admit it?"

"I didn't. I spent three weeks there, that's all, Ivy. Sorry, Michele, whatever your bloody name is now," Rhys objected. "Untie me. Get me out of here, Sam."

Sam stared at him, suddenly seeing him in a different light. Something about his demeanour had changed, making her question the trust she once had in him. "Nick, can you free Rhys?"

"Of course, boss."

Sam took a step back and watched as her three colleagues dealt with the two suspects and her fiancé.

A knife dropped to the floor—one Michele had concealed up her sleeve. Rhys would never realise how lucky he had been; Sam was sure of that.

It was over... or was it?

"Do you need medical care?" she asked Rhys.

He shook his head firmly. "No, they didn't hurt me. You rescued me before they got the chance."

Sam smiled, but inside, her stomach was churning. There was something in his smile that didn't sit comfortably with her. "Call for backup. We need to get the three of them transferred to the station ASAP."

"Wait, you want me to go to the station?" Rhys queried.

"Yes. You'll need to give us a statement."

His eyes narrowed. "Can't that wait? I've been held prisoner for a few days, and the first thing you want from me is a *statement*? I don't get it, Sam."

She shrugged and stood back into the shadows, confused by the emotions stirring within her.

Three patrol cars arrived. The suspects and Rhys were loaded into separate cars, and the convoy headed back to the station. Sam had the tech guy, Adam, sitting beside her during the journey. He kept silent, sensing she wasn't in the mood to hold a conversation with him.

At the station, Jason asked how she wanted to proceed with the suspects and Rhys.

"I'll interview the suspects in the morning, but I want to get Rhys's statement down now."

Her three colleagues stood in the background, probably wondering what the heck was going on.

Sam turned to face them, her smile catching each of them off guard. "You did good this evening, boys. I couldn't be prouder of you. Go on, off you go. We'll go over what has happened in the morning. Hopefully, Bob will be back with us, then."

"Are you sure you don't want me to hang around with you, boss?" Nick asked.

"No, it's fine. Go, I won't be long behind you."

Her colleagues reluctantly left the station. Jason, the desk sergeant, had put Rhys in an interview room. Sam collected two cups of coffee from the vending machine and went to see him.

"I still can't believe you're not allowing me to go home, Sam."

"I'm sorry. Had you needed medical care, this would have been delayed. I need to get down the facts of what happened while they're still fresh in your mind."

"What? That's insane, as if I'm likely to forget. Why are you treating me like a criminal? They abducted me and, I believe, had you not shown up, they would have killed me. I'm thankful for your intervention. I'll be forever in your debt."

"You're welcome. My team and I were only doing our jobs."

He stared at her, bewildered, and shook his head. "Have you heard yourself? I'm your fiancé, but you're treating me like a stranger. I want to know why."

Ignoring his question, she said, "Rhys, the quicker you start telling me how you were abducted and what happened during your time spent at the hands of those criminals, the sooner you can go home."

"You and not *we*? What does that mean? Aren't you coming with me?"

Her gaze dropped to her notebook. "No, I'll stay at the station tonight. I have two suspects I need to interview. Shall we get on?"

HALF AN HOUR LATER, Rhys finally finished telling her how he'd been abducted and the level of violence he had suffered at the hands of Penn and Turner. Sam arranged for a patrol car to drop Rhys home. She hated the way she felt, but until she had the chance to figure out her emotions, Sam knew she would struggle to be in the same room as him. Maybe she would feel differently once she had interviewed Penn and Turner, although she had grave reservations if that would be the case.

She spent the night at her desk, going over the facts and pulling together the missing pieces that she had discovered since they had made the arrests. Eventually, around three in the morning, after making copious notes for the upcoming interviews, she curled into her jacket, surrounded by empty coffee cups and plenty of ghosts, and fell asleep at her desk.

Sam always kept a change of clothes at work. After having a wash in the ladies' toilet, she returned to her office, ready for her day to begin. Rhys rang her mobile at seven and every fifteen minutes after that, until she finally accepted his call.

"Where have you been?"

"I've been busy in the interview room. Why?"

"Sam, why are you avoiding me?"

"I'm not. Sorry, I have to go now. I need to hold my morning meeting with the team. Enjoy your day."

"Sam... Sam..."

She ended the call and swallowed down the lump clogging her throat.

The only bright spark to Sam's morning was the fact that Bob had joined them. He knocked on the door to her office and poked his head in. "Good morning. Do you need a coffee?"

She tore out of her seat and kissed him on the cheek. "How are you?"

"No lasting damage done. I threatened to do all sorts to the doctor if he didn't release me."

"You didn't?"

He grinned. "You know me too well. No, I didn't, but I would have if he'd tried to keep me in. How are you?" He studied her warily.

"I'm fine. I think. I'll let you know once I've interviewed the suspects. You can't be involved. I'll get Nick to sit in with me, if that's all right?"

"I was about to suggest the same. No offence taken. It wouldn't be right for me to be there. Umm... are we all right, Sam?"

Her smile slipped. "I think so. I'm still trying to process everything that's happened."

"I know I shouldn't have to remind you—you're getting married in a few weeks. The quicker you get your head around things, the better.

How's Rhys? I was surprised that he didn't join me at the hospital. I asked the staff if he had been admitted; they told me there was nothing on the system."

"I think he's all right. He seemed so last night... when I took down his statement."

Bob's brow wrinkled. "You did what? Hang on just a second. You said you hadn't seen him since last night. That means either you came in super early this morning, or you never went home. Please don't tell me you spent the night here?"

Sam returned to her seat. "Guilty as charged. I'd rather not discuss it; my head's a mess."

"You need to talk to someone; otherwise, you won't be able to move on, Sam. Rhys wasn't to blame, nor was I, and yet you seem to have forgiven me. Or is that my imagination?"

Sam waved her hand from side to side. "I said I still have to work through my emotions. Can we talk about this later? I have two interviews I need to prepare for, and time is running out."

"Whatever. I'll tell Nick that he'll be required to sit in with you."

Guilt ripped through her for upsetting her partner after all he had been through in the last twenty-four hours. She watched him walk away, shoulders heavy with fatigue, and regret burned her chest like acid.

Half an hour later, notes in hand, Sam collected Nick, and they made their way downstairs.

"I appreciate you choosing me for this task, boss," Nick said without sounding too gushy.

"Consider it your initiation test. I'm kidding. I would normally have chosen either Liam or Oliver, but they've sat in on interviews before; you haven't. Hopefully, it'll help you settle in and appreciate your position on the team."

"I won't let you down. You're amazing. You've always put others before yourself. It hasn't gone unnoticed by me over the years; that's why I jumped at the chance to join your team."

"I'm delighted to have you on board, Nick. Let's see what the evil twins have to say."

"Blimey, are they related?"

"No, at least, I don't think they are. It was me fooling around. Who do you reckon we should speak to first?"

"The female."

"Good, that's what I thought as well. Right, will you do the honours and ask Jason to bring her in? I'll be in Interview Room One. The solicitor is ready and waiting for us."

Michele Turner entered the room, indignation rife in her eyes. Nick said the normal verbiage for the recording, then Sam asked her first question.

"Which do you prefer to be called, Ivy or Michele?"

"Whichever. You're not going to get anything out of me anyway, so it doesn't really matter, does it? Er... no comment."

Sam resisted the urge to roll her eyes and sigh. Instead, she fixed a smile in place and asked another ten questions, to which Turner gave the obligatory 'no comment'. Then Sam asked the officer at the back of the room to escort Michele back to her cell.

"I had a feeling it would go like this. The next suspect is an ex-copper. Will you be wanting a word with him before the interview begins, Miss Nyland?" Sam asked the duty solicitor.

"It might be a good idea, Inspector."

Sam and Nick took a ten-minute coffee break before returning to the room. She sat opposite Gareth Penn. His demeanour was entirely different to Turner's. Sam sensed he was going to be more forthcoming with his answers than his associate.

"Tell me, Mr Penn, when did you meet up with Michele Turner?"

"I can't remember the exact date. It must have been nearly twenty years ago, during the investigation into Pendle House. The longer the investigation went on, and the more times I met her, the more I knew we had an affinity for each other. Before you ask, there was never anything romantic between us. It was obvious pretty early on that the investigation would fail the minute I set foot in that place. It didn't take long for my DCI to warn me off. He told me to wrap things up early before they got a chance to get going. You know yourself what that's like, Inspector. To me, it was like a red rag to a bull. I spent the next two months going back and forth to the children's home under the pretext of wrapping up the investigation. Every time I went back, the hackles rose on my neck. My gut told me that the man in charge, Foster, was lying and that sinister things were happening there."

"I can only imagine the frustration you must have felt. Why didn't you take it higher?"

"Back in the day, there was a lot of corruption going on in the Force. If you do your research, the superintendent at the time, Morley, was on the take. He was brought down by another DCI and his team. The case of Pendle House got shoved to the side until things were deemed to have settled down. By then, it was too late. The children's home had already been classed as unsafe by the public, and the council finally grew some balls and shut it down."

"So justice was finally served."

"Hardly. That's when Ivy—sorry, Michele—and I decided to work together. I uncovered some secret files when Pendle closed down. Don't ask me how I gained access to the place. I'm sure you can figure that out yourself."

Sam raised an eyebrow. "Okay, can you tell me what was in the files?"

"Kids' names, the dates they arrived, the punishments they received and, in some cases, the manner in which they died."

"And you did nothing about it?" Sam queried, aghast.

He wagged his finger. "Don't sound so shocked. I tried, believe me. No one wanted to know. They told me to let it go after the home had closed its doors for the final time. I was ordered to bury it, except I couldn't. Night after night, I lay awake, imagining those innocent kids screaming as they were beaten black and blue. Some of the beatings were so harsh they led to several young girls dying. Answer me this: would you have walked away? Done nothing? Our job is to serve the community, not sit back when something as deplorable as this surfaces."

"Why has it taken you and Michele this long to start dishing out the justice if, as you say, it affected you the way it did?"

"Michele wanted to avenge their deaths earlier, but she's been ill.

She had cancer. Fortunately, being the fighter she is, she pulled through. She got in touch with me last year and said the time was right."

"Why kill Claire Owen, a member of my team?"

"She gained access to a file she shouldn't have, which effectively got the ball rolling. As soon as we knew a copper was digging into Pendle House, it was obvious we would need to come up with a plan to silence those involved, and quickly."

"Why couldn't you have just kidnapped and tortured them? That would have been bad enough, but to take their lives, especially Claire's. All she was doing was her job."

He shook his head. "She wasn't; it went deeper than that. Michele recognised her from a photo taken at the home. She helped out there as a child."

Sam shrugged. "So did a lot of people. We found the photo, the one you're referring to. There were a lot of other children wearing a uniform similar to Claire's. We assumed they were volunteers from a nearby school."

"Ah, yes. But the others didn't witness a beating first-hand. Claire did; she chose to say nothing."

Sam and Nick exchanged a concerned glance.

"She was just a child herself. What could she have done about it?"

"Spoken out. I don't have to tell you that there have been a lot of high-profile cases of abuse over the years. The people who have remained silent are just as much to blame as the abusers themselves. Don't you agree?"

He had a point. Which was why, deep down, Sam was struggling to forgive Rhys.

"I've got you thinking about that now, haven't I?" Penn said.

"You have, simply because none of it makes any sense: the length of time you've waited, the manner in which you chose to silence, or should I say kill, your victims; the way you kidnapped Rhys but kept him alive. Why?"

"Because Michele had plans for him."

"Such as?"

"No comment."

That's where the interview effectively ended, because every question Sam asked after that was met with the same response. She nodded for Nick to end the interview, and Penn was returned to his cell.

The rest of the day was spent with the team, filling in the necessary paperwork for the CPS and tying up any loose ends.

EPILOGUE

Two weeks later, the sky over Cumbria was brighter and calmer, although the storm raging inside Sam refused to pass. She'd had a lot to consider recently.

Knowing that another two serial killers were now on remand, awaiting trial, should have improved her mood. It hadn't, far from it. The media attention was doing little to put the case to bed either. She was constantly being bombarded by calls from journalists, both local and national, which were taking up too much of her time and wearing on her sanity.

Her relationship with Bob had changed, despite her initial welcome back speech once he'd returned to work. He'd noticed her attitude towards him had altered, and he had been busy bending her ear about it at every available opportunity for the past two weeks.

Things weren't faring better at home between her and Rhys either. He was quieter. In truth, they both were. He'd decided it would be a good idea to move into the spare room, giving her the space she needed to come to terms with how she felt. He was still sleeping with the lights on, a clear indication of how deeply he'd been affected by his abduction. She wanted to be there for him, but the shutters remained firmly closed.

Today she had booked a day off from work. Rhys had suggested he take time off so they could spend the day together, but she'd told him that she'd prefer some time alone.

She had a lot to figure out, such as what she intended to do with the next stage of her life. She had brought her fancy notebook with her to a place close to her heart: Coniston Water. She had found a secluded spot, away from the crowds, and settled on a log overlooking the famous lake, with Tilly by her side, her chin resting on Sam's feet. There, pen in hand, Sam wrote her letter of resignation.

She rewrote it several times until she was finally happy with the outcome. She didn't have it in her anymore to chase serial killers or to put her family and those she loved through the torture and torment caused by her chosen career.

Something had changed in her during this particular investigation—a nagging voice in her head telling her to reassess the decisions she'd made in life and to alter things for the better. She needed to put herself first, for a change, at the risk of upsetting those around her.

The last couple of years had proven that life was too short, and if she didn't enjoy it, she'd grow old and have regrets. She glanced down at her dog; she wasn't Sonny, but she was bonding with the sweet pup now. She had rescued Tilly from a life on the streets, and in return, little Tilly had given her so much more. For a start, the incentive to live her dreams. To say sod it to everything and do what was right for her and her four-legged companion.

She tore off the resignation letter and popped it into an envelope which she addressed to DCI Armstrong.

Now she had one more letter she needed to write—to Rhys. As far as she was concerned, once the trust had been broken between them, she couldn't see a way back. Although she admitted that he wasn't to blame for anything that had happened at Pendle House, the fact remains that he had neglected to tell her about that part of his past, and that was what really hurt her the most. He had led her to believe that there were no skeletons in his closet, which had turned out to be a major lie. How could she ever trust him again? It was like living with Chris all over again. The lies and deceit didn't belong in a relationship.

Crystal was going to be livid to hear the news that the wedding was off, but *c'est la vie*. Hopefully, in time, her sister would be able to forgive her and understand her reasons for calling it off.

She didn't care if Rhys understood or not, as harsh as that sounded. People needed to show their partners respect in all aspects of their life. Trust and loyalty in Sam's eyes were everything in a marriage, and without that...

Tears dripped onto the sheet of paper as she said her final farewell to Rhys. She had booked a cottage in Pooley Bridge for a few days. That would give him time to pack up his things and move out.

Doreen was going to be flabbergasted by her decision. Sam hoped that, in time, her elderly neighbour would understand.

She ended the note with a kiss, more out of habit than anything else, and put it in the envelope. Then, after a much-needed hug from Tilly, she got back on the road and drove to Rhys's office. Coward that she was, she handed the letter to Brenda.

Confused, Brenda took it and asked if Sam was all right.

"I will be. It was nice knowing you."

She left the office and returned to the car. This time she headed towards the station, where she dropped the letter off at reception, then drove home. She packed a small suitcase, gathered all of Tilly's bits together and drove to the cottage.

The owner welcomed her and showed her around the property. Katherine left her to enjoy her stay. Sam rested her head against the door, wondering whether she had in fact, done the right thing.

"No regrets, girl. You've got this. It's time for you to get on with your life. Just you, the open road and your little dog, Tilly, by your side."

THE END

A Note from the Author

As I close the final chapter on DI Sam Cobbs' journey, I want to take a moment to thank *you*, dear reader, for coming along for the ride.

This series has explored some of life's darkest corners—loss, betrayal, justice and survival—but at its heart, it has always been about strength: the strength to face the truth, to carry on after heartbreak, and to make impossible choices in the name of what's right.

DI Sam Cobbs has grown through every case, every wound, every whispered doubt—and now, she's chosen to walk away from the job that defined her, stepping into an uncertain future with courage, a loyal dog by her side and a heart still healing.

I hope Sam has touched you as much as she's stayed with me. Whether you've followed her from book one or met her more recently, I'm so grateful for your support, your messages and your shared love of a good thriller with heart.

Though Sam's story ends here (for now), the truth will always find its way out—and there are always more stories to tell.

Thank you from the bottom of my heart for reading.

With love,

Mel xx

THANK you for reading The Truth Will Out. If you've enjoyed Sam's final adventure, please consider leaving a review on Amazon.

ALSO, while I have your attention, have you read any of my other fast-paced crime thrillers yet?

WHY NOT TRY the first book in the DI Sara Ramsey series
No Right To Kill

. . .

OR GRAB the first book in the bestselling, award-winning, Justice series here, Cruel Justice

OR THE FIRST book in the spin-off Justice Again series, Gone in Seconds

PERHAPS YOU'D PREFER to try one of my other police procedural series, the DI Kayli Bright series which begins with The Missing Children

OR MAYBE YOU'D enjoy the DI Sally Parker series set in Norfolk, Wrong Place

OR MY GRITTY police procedural starring DI Nelson set in Manchester, Torn Apart

OR MAYBE YOU'D like to try one of my successful psychological thrillers I know The Truth or She's Gone or Shattered Lives

ALSO BY M A COMLEY

She's Gone (A psychological thriller)

Shattered Lives (A psychological thriller)

Evil In Disguise – a novel based on True events

Deadly Act (Hero series novella)

Torn Apart (Hero series #1)

End Result (Hero series #2)

In Plain Sight (Hero Series #3)

Double Jeopardy (Hero Series #4)

Criminal Actions (Hero Series #5)

Regrets Mean Nothing (Hero series #6)

Prowlers (Di Hero Series #7)

Sole Intention (Intention series #1)

Grave Intention (Intention series #2)

Devious Intention (Intention #3)

Cozy mysteries

Murder at the Wedding

Murder at the Hotel

Murder by the Sea

Death on the Coast

Death By Association

Merry Widow (A Lorne Simpkins short story)

It's A Dog's Life (A Lorne Simpkins short story)

A Time To Heal (A Sweet Romance)

A Time For Change (A Sweet Romance)

High Spirits

The Temptation series (Romantic Suspense/New Adult Novellas)

Past Temptation

Lost Temptation

Clever Deception (co-written by Linda S Prather)

Tragic Deception (co-written by Linda S Prather)

Sinful Deception (co-written by Linda S Prather)

KEEP IN TOUCH WITH M A COMLEY

Newsletter
http://smarturl.it/8jtcvv

BookBub
www.bookbub.com/authors/m-a-comley

Blog
http://melcomley.blogspot.com

Facebook Readers' Page
https://www.facebook.com/groups/2498593423507951

TikTok
https://www.tiktok.com/@melcomley

Printed in Dunstable, United Kingdom

67637201R00117